D1467793

The Etruscan Smile

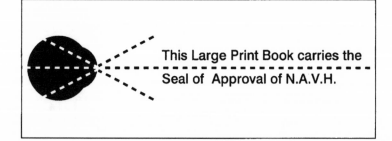

The Etruscan Smile

Velda Johnston

Thorndike Press • Thorndike, Maine

Published in 2000 by arrangement with Spectrum Literary Agency.

Thorndike Large Print ® Candlelight Series.

The tree indicium is a trademark of Thorndike Press.

The text of this Large Print edition is unabridged.
Other aspects of the book may vary from the original edition.

Set in 16 pt. Plantin.

Printed in the United States on permanent paper.

Library of Congress Cataloging-in-Publication Data

Johnston, Velda.
    The Etruscan smile : a novel of suspense / Velda Johnston.
        p. cm.
    ISBN 0-7862-2449-5 (lg. print : hc : alk. paper)
    1. Americans — Travel — Italy — Tuscany —
Fiction. 2. Missing persons — Italy — Tuscany —
Fiction. 3. Archaeologists — Italy — Tuscany —
Fiction. 4. Tuscany (Italy) — Fiction. 5. Large type
books. I. Title.
PS3560.O394 E87 2000
813'.54—dc21   99-088725

*For Emily Cobb, and also
for Benjie, Simon, Charity,
and Henrietta*

1

The ancient farmhouse had an empty look. As I drove my rented Simca onto the bare yard, I felt a shriveling of the hope that had sustained me during the long night flight from New York, a hope that I would find that Althea was not missing, after all.

I shut off the engine. Then I sat there for a moment, looking at the house, with its reddish-yellow bricks hand-fashioned more than three centuries ago from the Tuscan earth, and at the two openings, wide and now doorless, on the ground floor. The early afternoon sunlight was so bright that I could see only blackness beyond those openings. From Althea's letters, though, I knew that the generations of Italian peasants who had lived here used to keep their animals on the ground floor — milk cows, and sheep, and the long-horned white oxen who drew their wooden plows.

I became aware that Caesar, sitting patiently beside me, had begun to pant. I looked at his lolling tongue, his tawny head brushing the little car's top. Despite my anxiety over Althea, I felt a stab of compassion for Caesar. He must have found the last fifteen hours or so an ordeal. First there was the crate which had confined him in the hold of a 747. Then the noisy confusion at Milan's airport where, at the car rental desk, I had arranged for the Simca. Then the drive south in the cramped little car, past fields and vineyards that seemed to shimmer in the late June heat.

I opened the car door. "Come on, fella." The German shepherd padded beside me as I passed the old well with its high brick coping and then went around the corner of the house. I had never seen this house before. I had never even been in Italy before. And yet, from Althea's vivid and detailed letters, as well as from the color slides she had sent me, I knew that I would find a doorless entryway at this side of the house, and a wooden staircase leading up to the living quarters.

I hesitated for a moment at the stairs' foot, looking up through the dimness. Then, with Caesar's toenails clicking behind me over the worn steps, I climbed to the age-blackened oak door at the top. I knocked, and then called, "Althea?" hoping against hope that I would hear quick footsteps, and that the door would open, and I would see my sister standing there, tall and

8

red-haired and beautiful.

Except for Caesar's panting breath, nothing but silence.

In our grandparents' house in that little upstate New York town, the front door key had been kept above the lintel. I reached up. Almost immediately my groping fingers found it, a heavy iron key almost six inches long.

It turned in the lock with a grating sound. I stepped into a room whose every detail I knew well from all the times I had held a color-slide viewer up to the light and admired this floor of dark red tile, the tall terra-cotta heating stove, the cavernous fireplace, and the rectangular dining table and chairs of some dark wood. But in the color slides the dark red floor had been lustrous, the fireplace and irons freshly blackened, the potted geraniums on the deep windowsills a healthy pink. The geraniums were dead and shriveled stalks now. And a layer of dust covered the furniture and the floor, a layer heavy enough that footprints showed distinctly on the red tile. For a glad moment I thought, "At least she's been back here recently!" Then I realized that they were the footprints of a man — no, two men.

Policemen. I recalled the Contessa

Rafaello's voice, now swelling and now fading across the transatlantic wire as I sat, stunned and incredulous, in my Manhattan apartment two nights before. "She has been missing for more than two months, Miss Develin. At first we did not worry. Your sister is often away for days at a time. But until now she has never failed to make her rent payment promptly, either leaving the check in the postbox at the foot of our drive, or, if she were away, mailing it to us. And so we fear that something may have happened —"

Her voice had faded for a few seconds. Then I heard, "— post office in the village says she left no forwarding address. So I thought it best to ask overseas information for your number. I have notified the carabinieri in Isolotta — that is the nearest village — and they have searched the farmhouse and its surroundings thoroughly. They even probed the well." As if realizing the implications of that last sentence, she stopped speaking for a moment, and then added hurriedly, "They found no trace of her."

They had found no trace. And so they had left, after first replacing the key on the shelf above the door.

Caesar whined deep in his throat.

Quickly I crossed the room to the ancient stone sink and took down two brown earthenware bowls from the long shelf above it. Grasping the handle of the pump attached to the stone sinkboard, I worked it up and down vigorously. For perhaps a minute the pump made dry, asthmatic sounds. Then the water gushed out. I remembered one of the first of Althea's letters from Italy, written about seven years before. "I sold three pictures last month — three! — and so I asked the Rafaellos for permission to put in some modern improvements. They said yes, as why shouldn't they, since it's their property I'm improving. But anyway, I'll soon have a bathroom in what has been a second sleeping room. No more chilly trips through the dark to the outhouse — in fact, I'll have that quaint structure razed — and no more baths in a tin tub set in the middle of my kitchen-dining-living room floor. I'll have a gas stove with bottled gas, and so no more cooking in the fireplace unless I want to. Already I've installed a pump in the sink. The blasted thing works so hard that it's almost as much effort as carrying water up from the well, but I'm sure it's fine for firming the upper arms and what Grandmother Rossi calls the bust."

11

I placed a bowl of water on the floor. Then I went down to my rented car and took my suitcase from the trunk. I was about to turn back to the house when I noticed the mailbox, affixed to its wooden support there at the road's edge. I hurried to it and looked inside. Nothing.

When I had climbed back up the stairs, I found Caesar still lapping water. I took a package of dry dog food from my suitcase, spilled some of its contents into the second bowl, and added water from the pump. Eagerly Caesar transferred his attention to the food.

The air in the dusty room seemed stifling. I crossed to the double windows on the opposite side from the bare yard, unlatched them, and pushed them wide. Directly below, on a brick-floored terrace, stood a white wrought-iron table and two matching chairs. More dead plants stood in pots along the low terrace coping. "I am making a terrace," Althea had written me four or five years before, "out of what was once the farm's threshing floor. I'm laying most of the bricks myself."

Beyond the terrace the land sloped gently toward a river that appeared to be about a half mile away. Undoubtedly the land between the house and the stream once had been under cultivation. Now it was a tangle of tall grass and scarlet poppies, studded here and there with gnarled olive trees, their silver-green leaves motionless in the still air. Beyond the stream rose gently rolling hills. Because Althea had sent me photographs that must have been taken from this very window, I knew that the hillside villa I could see far in the distance, its terra cotta towers visible above tall cypress, belonged to the Rafaellos, owners of this old house and the two hundred acres surrounding it.

And on a hilltop somewhere beyond the Rafaello villa, I knew, was the fifteenth-century walled village in which both my grandparents, my mother's parents, had been born.

How I had looked forward to the day when I would be here with Althea, standing at this window and looking out at the lovely Tuscan landscape her letters had described. Ever since she had gone to Italy and decided to stay there, I had longed to join her, at least for a few months. In fact, perhaps that was why when I was graduated from college two years before I had abandoned my idea of seeking a job in advertising and instead had gone to work as an English teacher in a private prep school in Manhattan. Teachers, after all, get the summer off.

Last April I had written to her, saying that I had saved enough money to come to Italy. There had been no reply to my air-mail letter, nor to a second one I had sent. Puzzled as well as hurt, because it was unlike Althea to ignore my letters, I had tried to tell myself that she was busy with her painting, perhaps even a commissioned painting, and that I would hear from her soon.

Now, thinking of those letters, I stood rigid. Where were they? They had not been returned to me. They were not in her mailbox. They had not been forwarded to whatever place she had gone. According to the Contessa, Althea had given the post office no forwarding address.

I thought of someone secretly visiting that mailbox each day, or more likely each night, and removing its contents. Someone who had not wanted the mail carrier to report to his superiors that Althea Develin's mail was piling up, lest they tell the carabinieri, and they in turn notify Althea's grandparents in Oak Corners, New York, or her sister in Manhattan.

Suddenly this old house, made beautiful by Althea's taste and work and hard-earned money, no longer seemed a pleasant place. Instead I had a sense of a silent vibration in the hot air between these ancient walls, like a memory trace of something dark and secret that had happened here.

After a moment the feeling passed. But I stayed there at the window, hands pressed on the sill, somehow reluctant to turn and look at the dusty room behind me.

"Hey! Althea? Is that you up there?"

I whirled around. The voice, a man's, had come from the foot of the stairs. Caesar raised his head from the bowl and moved, stiff-legged and bristling, toward the half-opened door. I hurried across the room, put a calming hand on his head, and opened the door wide. The man stood at the foot of the stairs, wide-shouldered body dark against the brilliant sunlight outside, up-turned face indistinct in the stairwell's dimness.

He said, "Who the devil are *you?*" His voice was English. Not smooth, BBC, Oxford-Cambridge English. Some sort of regional accent.

I answered, "Who the devil are you?" Sensing my annoyance, Caesar barked, and then growled deep in his throat. I said, "It's all right, Caesar," although I was by no means sure it was.

"The name's Jeffrey Hale."

"I'm Samantha Develin."

"Althea's sister?" He started up the stairs.

"Wait!" I did not want him in the house, a man whose face I had not seen clearly. "I'll come down."

"As you like." He turned and went out into the sunlight. I descended, comforted by the click of Caesar's claws over the steps behind me.

The man, wearing chinos and a light-weight blue pullover, waited just outside the doorway. He was in his early thirties, I guessed, and about five-feet-ten-inches tall. Seen from above, those wide shoulders had made him appear shorter.

He stared at me. "You can't be her sister. Althea's how old? At least thirty-five, probably more. And you're what? Twenty?"

I saw no reason to tell this stranger my age, which was twenty-three. "I'm twelve years younger than Althea."

Again Caesar gave that low growl. Jeffrey Hale looked down at him and said, "He doesn't like me, does he?" His gaze returned to my face. "Or is it that he senses you don't like me?"

At least this man knew something about dogs. I looked at him appraisingly. He wore his curly brown hair fairly short. His face, blunt-featured and deeply tanned, was made arresting by the bluest eyes I had ever seen, not dark blue eyes, but the clear, brilliant blue of star sapphires.

I answered, "He knows that you startled me, that's all."

"Sorry about that." When I didn't speak, he went on, "Is Althea on her way back here?"

My throat tightened up. "I don't know."

"Where the hell is she? Milan?"

I said wretchedly, "I don't know. Maybe no one does."

He said after a moment, "Do you want to talk to me about it?"

I hesitated. He went on, "I know. You know nothing about me. But I've been a neighbor of your sister's for the last five summers. I rent part of a house about three miles down the road. The rest of the year I teach archaeology at an English university near Nottingham. Probably you've never heard of it."

So we had something in common. True, I had only a bachelor of arts degree, and he probably had a string of letters after his name, but at least we were both teachers.

"There's table and chairs around on the

terrace. We could sit —"

"Not on those wrought-iron chairs, unless we want blistered rears. The coping would be better."

As we moved toward the terrace, I saw a bicycle leaning against the wall of the house. So that was how he had approached this place so silently.

Across one section of the terrace coping an orange tree, hung with greenish fruit, cast motionless shadow. We sat there, with Caesar lying on the red bricks close to my feet. Head sunk on his paws, he was quiet now, but kept his alert brown eyes fixed upon the Englishman.

Jeffrey Hale said, "When did you last hear from your sister?"

"Sometime in late March." I was about to mention those two unanswered letters, but a thought stopped me. This man, this "neighbor," pedaling down the narrow road at night, stopping at that untended mailbox —

"I've been worried," I said, "but I couldn't call her. She has no phone."

"No, or electricity either. It would cost a pretty penny to have phone and power lines brought in, and I can't imagine the Rafaellos paying for it. They're just holding onto this land in hopes of selling it to the city of Florence as an airport." He paused. "How is it you decided to come here?"

I told him about the transatlantic call from Isobel Rafaello, the Contessa. He said dryly, "Could it be that Althea hasn't sent them the rent? Could that be what drew their attention?"

"She did say something about the rent." I added, "What is she like?" Much as I wanted to hear what he had to say about Althea, I needed to know about the Contessa too. As soon as I had bathed and changed my travel-wrinkled dark green pants suit for something more presentable, I intended to visit the Rafaellos.

"The Contessa? Late forties, handsome enough, and twice as haughty as if she came from a long line of titled aristocrats."

"But doesn't she? After all, a contessa —"

"Her husband — he's dead now — was made a papal count a few years ago."

"Oh!" After a moment I asked, "How does one become a papal count?"

"By giving enough money to the Vatican, I suppose."

I stiffened. He said, "What's the matter? Are you Catholic?"

"Not really, although I was baptized and

confirmed as a Catholic." Here in this beautiful but alien place, I felt a stab of nostalgia at the thought of Oak Corners, and church bells pealing as my grandparents and my big sister and I, in Sunday best, moved along cracked sidewalks through cool, early morning sunlight. "But anyway, I don't think one should be cynical about religious matters."

"Why do people confuse realism with cynicism? And what's wrong with being rewarded for giving to some cause? Men become ambassadors that way. Others get their names on stained-glass windows in Baptist churches, and others become papal counts." He grinned. "As for me, my people back in Yorkshire have been Chapel for generations — what I suppose you would call Methodists. Very egalitarian and all that. But even so, I've noticed that the families that give most to the Chapel are assigned the front pews."

"I suppose so." Then, eager to bring the conversation back to Althea: "You mentioned Milan. Why do you think my sister may have gone there?"

He said after a moment, "Because she often does go there for a few days."

"But not for weeks at a time?"

"Not as far as I know."

"Why does she go there?"

"I don't know."

He had said it a little too quickly. After a moment I asked, "How well do you know Althea?"

"Quite well."

"Are you — Have you been her lover?" He gave me a startled look. "You can tell me." My voice was cold. "I'm not a child."

"Very well. As you Americans say, we did have a little thing going the first summer I was here."

"What happened?"

He shrugged. "Her attention turned — elsewhere."

Something in his tone told me that he meant more than one elsewhere. Well, from the time I had been old enough to take an interest in such matters I had guessed that Althea led a varied love life. But I had also been aware that she was beautiful, talented, kind, and generous. And I adored her.

I thought of Saturday afternoons when I was fourteen or fifteen, and my friends gathered at my house to play records and dance. Althea, home for the weekend from her glamorous commercial artist's job in glamorous Manhattan, needed only to walk through the living room to bring a stunned, silly look to the face of every boy there.

Somehow I had never been jealous of her. For one thing, I knew that these boys, a dozen years her junior, had about as much chance with her as I would have with Robert Redford. And also, as I have said, I adored her.

All through my high school years she had kept promising me that when I too went to New York to attend N.Y.U., I could live with her. But before I was ready for college, she had sold several pictures and had decided to go to Italy to paint "for a few months." She had never come back. When I did go to New York and enrolled at N.Y.U., I shared an apartment with two girls — a living room with a studio couch, a twin-bedded bedroom, and a bathroom perennially festooned with bras and panty-hose.

Jeffrey Hale was watching me, blue eyes narrowed. He said, "I still can't believe you are Althea's sister."

"Why? Is it still because of the difference in our ages? There was a child in between, a boy, but he lived only a few days."

"No, I didn't mean just the difference in your ages."

I felt I could see myself through his eyes.

Slight, a little below medium height. Hair neither blond nor brown — the sort I call hair-colored hair — instead of any sister's luxuriant dark-red mane. Hazel eyes rather than Althea's changeable ones, which were sometimes blue, sometimes almost green, according to what she wore.

"I know I don't look like her," I said somewhat stiffly, "and I know I look younger than I am. People with small faces usually do."

He ignored that. "I think you ought to go home. You say the Rafaellos have already notified the carabinieri in Isolotta. They're in touch with the police throughout Italy, and in other countries too, when they need to be. Let them find her. See the local carabinieri, if you want to, and then go home."

"Go home!" I felt astonished and angry. "Without knowing where my sister is? I intend staying right here until I find out."

Those brilliant eyes studied me. "How long is it since you saw Althea?"

"Seven years."

"A woman can change a lot in seven years, especially an American woman in Italy."

What was he trying to tell me? Of course

23

Althea probably looked older now, although I found it impossible to imagine her appearance altered in any way. Her character could not have changed, though. If it had, the change would have been apparent in her letters.

But her letters had been less frequent these past two years, I recalled uneasily. And although as loving as ever in tone, they had been much shorter. After a couple of paragraphs they were apt to end with, "No more for now, Samantha darling. Must get back to work." And certainly it was more than two years since she had suggested that I visit her.

"Anyway," Jeffrey Hale said, "I don't think your sister is in any trouble. I think she just decided to go off on a — To go off on a trip somewhere."

What had he been about to say? That he thought she'd gone off on a fling? A bender? Surely not the latter. Althea didn't drink.

"Are you trying to tell me my sister has turned into a lush?"

"Lord, no. At least I've never seen any evidence of it. In fact, she once told me that she found life far too interesting to blur it with alcohol."

Yes, that sounded like Althea. "Then

what did you mean when you said she had changed?"

"Just that people, even sisters, grow apart. At least from my impression of you so far, it's hard for me to imagine you two having anything in common." He hurried on, as if afraid I might ask him to enlarge upon that. "And I don't think you should stay alone here."

"Althea does. Besides, I've got Caesar."

At the sound of his name, Caesar lifted his massive head. A five-months-old puppy when I first saw him, he had grown into the largest shepherd I had ever seen.

Caesar had been part of the deal by which, after I graduated from both N.Y.U. and that apartment with the laundry-cluttered bathroom, I had obtained a sub-lease on what had been advertised as a "garden apartment" on West Twelfth Street. It was really a basement apartment, one long room with a tiny window high up on one wall, plus a tiny bathroom and kitchenette. There were glass doors, though, opening out onto a fenced-in yard, most of it paved, but with a few discouraged-looking rosebushes growing along one side.

The tenant, a California-bound girl in her mid-twenties, said that I could have the place for eight months for just what she paid — "I won't charge for the use of my furniture" — if I would take care of her dog.

Long before the eight months were up, I had resolved not to surrender Caesar. I would plead with his owner, offer her tempting sums. I even entertained dark schemes of taking him to a kennel, reporting to her that he had disappeared, and then moving to some place in Queens, no matter how remote from my job, where he would have a fenced-in area for exercise.

It was not just his beauty and intelligence that enchanted me. When I moved along the Greenwich Village Streets with Caesar, I feared no muggers. No cars stopped beside me at the curb, front door swinging open in invitation. And when on Saturdays I walked past construction sites where hardhats labored for princely sums in overtime, none of them even dared whistle.

A month before my sub-lease was up, Caesar's owner called me long distance. She was getting married to a Californian, and would not return to New York. I could buy her furniture for whatever I thought it was worth, and I could keep the apartment permanently, if I would take her dog along with it.

He had been all mine ever since. After I received that frightening phone call from Isobel Rafaello, I did not even consider leaving Caesar in a kennel. After all, I didn't know how long I would be gone. And perhaps, even then, I had sensed I might need his protection —

Jeffrey Hale eyed the shepherd, who looked steadily back at him. "Yes, you have Caesar." He added, "I don't think he's made up his mind about me yet."

That makes two of us, I thought. "Have you stopped by here often in the past few weeks?"

"Three or four times. I'd walk around to the terrace — she often paints out here — and then climb the stairs and knock. There was never any answer."

I looked at the plants, dead and shriveled in their pots set along the coping. "It's a pity you or someone else didn't think to water those plants. She'll be upset to find them dead."

"Why should she? She let them die. They've been like that since last summer."

I felt bewildered dismay. Perhaps my sister really had changed a great deal. Certainly it was strange that she would have nurtured geraniums into the healthy blooms of those color slides, and then

27

become too careless — or too taken up with other matters — to keep them alive.

I said, "Please excuse me now. I must go to see the Rafaellos."

"Better let me show you where to turn. I'll strap my bike on top of your car and ride along with you for a ways."

"But I'm not leaving just now. I need to freshen up." Besides, I had not even looked into the bedroom yet. Something there might give me a hint as to where she had gone.

"Take your time." He drew a small rolled-up magazine in a blue cover from the hip pocket of his chinos. As he un-rolled it, I saw the title, *The Archaeological Review*. He added, "I'll stay down here and read until you're ready."

"I may be quite some time, at least half an hour."

"That's all right, Samantha. I've been wanting to read this, anyway." Then: "What is it? Don't you like my using your first name?"

"It's just that I'm surprised. I always thought the English were more formal."

He grinned. "I'm one of the new En-glishmen. We don't carry umbrellas, we call girls birds or dollies, and if we don't naturally have an accent like David Frost's, we try to cultivate it."

I eyed him for a moment. "Then what are you, actually? The son of a belted earl?"

"No, I'm the real article. My father is a sheep farmer, I went to council school until I was ten and then to a third-rate boarding school, and then to London University. All strictly non-U. Now take your shower, or whatever."

"All right." With Caesar following, I left the terrace.

2

Upstairs I lingered in the kitchen for a few moments, noticing things that had escaped my attention earlier. The seat cushions, covered in red-and-white-checked cotton, on the old ladder-back chairs drawn up to the dining table. The carving knives in a rack above the stone sinkboard. The gas stove with its attached cylinder of butane. Evidently Althea did not trust that stove, for near it on the wall hung a red fire extinguisher. In one corner stood a pantry cupboard, its green painted doors decorated with flower decals. Near it was an old-fashioned brown wooden icebox.

I picked up my suitcase from the floor and carried it into the bedroom. Here too the floor was of red tile, its dust marked with the carabinieri's footprints. I looked at the three-quarter bed, with its old headboard made of some dark wood and elaborately carved with a grape leaf design, and its spread of blue monk's cloth. Against one wall stood a marble-topped dressing table, holding a lipstick caddy, a silver comb-and-brush set, and two bottles of perfume. Near it was a bureau, also marble-topped. A tall old wardrobe, of the same dark wood as the headboard but with its paneled doors uncarved, stood against an adjoining wall. Above the bed hung one of Althea's landscapes. Another picture stood, unfinished, on an easel near the window.

I opened the wardrobe's door. The meagerness of its contents did not surprise me. One long white dress, a Mexican wedding dress of fine cotton, with deep cuffs of lace on the elbow-length sleeves. One yellow pants suit made of a lightweight synthetic material. One winter-weight coat of green wool, and a tan raincoat. The rest of the hangers held pants or skirts. For a beautiful woman, Althea always had been remarkably uninterested in clothes.

I turned to the bureau. The top drawer, in addition to the usual jumble of hair curlers, bobby pins, and all-but-empty lipsticks, held a powerful-looking flashlight. The two lower drawers were filled with blouses, sweaters, and underclothing.

She could not have taken much with her. Even her raincoat had been left behind.

I thrust aside the disturbing implications of that thought. Althea was the sort who traveled light. And she probably

31

owned a second raincoat.

I started toward the bathroom's open door, and then stopped to look at the photographs on the marble-topped lamp table beside the bed. There was my college graduation picture in a lucite frame. Next to it was the familiar enlarged snapshot of our parents, Mary and Donald Develin, standing beside a Jaguar. It was the car in which, on the way home from a sports car rally, they had rolled over and over down a hillside to their deaths. That had happened only weeks after that picture was taken. How young they looked in the photograph! But then, they had been quite young, both of them about Althea's present age.

. The third photograph showed Luigi and Rosa Rossi, the grandparents who had raised Althea from the age of thirteen and me from the age of eight months. I recalled Althea posing them for that color snap, one day about a year before she went to Italy, in the back yard of our house in Oak Corners. Both thin and olive-skinned and gray-haired, they sat in metal-armed lawn chairs flanking the round cement birdbath. How happy they looked in that picture, how pleased that their beautiful red-haired granddaughter, "the artist," had traveled from New York to spend the weekend with us.

As I looked at those beloved faces, my heart twisted with guilt. The morning after receiving the Contessa's call, I had telephoned my grandparents to tell them that I had a reservation on that night's flight to Milan. I did not tell them, of course, that Althea was missing. Instead I said that she had invited me to stay with her for a few weeks. That, of course, was true — except that she had stopped issuing such invitations more than two years before.

I had expected my grandparents to be surprised by my abrupt decision, and even a little upset. What I had not expected was frantic opposition. What of the summer courses I had planned to take toward a possible master's degree? How could I think of taking my dog across the Atlantic "all-a nailed up in a box"? And Italy was a dangerous country now. People shooting each other in the streets, people getting kidnapped. Alternating with each other on the phone, speaking sometimes in Italian, sometimes in English that was still heavily accented despite their more than a half century in America, they begged me to at least visit them and talk it over before I left. After all, I could fly to Milan

Friday or Saturday.

Unwilling to burden them with the real reason for my hasty departure, I replied weakly that seats on transatlantic flights were already scarce, now that summer was here, and besides, flying on weekends was much more expensive.

Now I again wondered at their distress. Did they fear that I, like Althea, would find Italy so enchanting that I would stay here? Perhaps. But I had an uneasy sense that their reason had been more urgent than that. Unlikely as it sounded, I almost had the impression that they knew, or had guessed, something about Althea's situation that I myself did not know.

I turned away from the nightstand, lifted my suitcase onto the bed, and opened it. A pair of light blue pants and a matching overblouse on my arm, I went to the wardrobe and hung the garments up. Evidently my actions had conveyed to Caesar that we were to settle down here for a while, because he stretched out on the white shag rug beside the bed. I took a yellow terry cloth robe from my suitcase and went into the bathroom.

The tub was practically a museum piece, nearly six feet long and encased in dark wood. With her sure taste, Althea evidently had felt that a modern bathroom, all chrome and pastel-colored tile and fixtures, would strike a jarring note in this old farmhouse. It must have taken her considerable effort to find that tub. And when she did, it might well have cost her more than some shiny new product of a Milan factory.

Again I thought of those dead geraniums. How could Althea, after lavishing thought and work and money on this place, have allowed those plants to die? What made it even more inexplicable was that she had always been so tender of vulnerable living things, whether plants, or animals, or humans. My grandparents had often recounted how Althea, the most popular girl in her high school class, always invited to her parties the classmates that everyone else ignored — the fat boy who stuttered, the cross-eyed girl, the twin boys whose father spent about a third of his time in the town lock-up for public drunkenness.

And yet, as if neither they nor their surroundings mattered any longer, she had allowed her once-cherished plants to die of thirst. She hadn't even removed their withered remains from the pots.

I looked at the pump standing at the

faucet-end of the tub. Evidently here, as in the kitchen, one had to work to bring water up from the well. I turned on the faucet, and then pumped the handle up and down until water gushed forth. Testing it with my hand, I found it at first almost warm. Rapidly it grew colder. In the winter, undoubtedly, Althea carried heated water from the kitchen stove to the tub. But in weather like this, a tepid bath would be welcome.

Ten minutes later, swathed in the terry robe, I returned to the bedroom. When I had dressed in blue pants and blouse, now free of wrinkles, I moved over to the unfinished picture on the easel. For several minutes I looked at it, puzzled. The subject did not bewilder me. From photographs I had seen, I knew that this was an unfinished painting of Giotto's Tower in Florence. But the technique, an almost photograph realism, was unlike that of any of Althea's paintings I had seen in the past.

I turned and looked at the painting above the bed. That one I instantly would have recognized as my sister's work, no matter where I had seen it. The paint was laid on so thickly that if I walked close to it, I knew, the picture would appear like a jumbled, multi-colored relief map. It was only at this distance that one could see that she had painted a tangled old garden of poppies and lupins and marguerites, shimmering in the sunlight.

I turned back to the unfinished picture on the easel. The paint lay flat on the canvas. The vertical lines of the tower might have been drawn with a ruler. Well, maybe Canaletto had replaced the French Impressionists as a major influence in her work. I hoped not. Perhaps the painting would look different when it was finished, but right now it struck me as commonplace and dull.

I looked down through the window. Jeffrey Hale still sat on the terrace coping, magazine in hand, one chino-clad leg crossed over the other knee. I picked up my shoulder bag and, followed by Caesar, went to the door and locked it behind us. As I went down the stairs, I dropped that heavy old key into my bag.

3

The Simca, with the Englishman in the back seat, his bike in the luggage carrier on the roof, and Caesar beside me, moved down the narrow road past gently sloping vineyards. From one of the books about Italy which I had read — and I began reading such books almost as soon as Althea took up residence here — I knew that in Virgil's time the Tuscan farmers espaliered their grapevines between mulberry trees. They still did. The vines stretched between the gnarled trunks, their unripe clusters, if any, hidden among the big, dull green leaves.

I looked into the rear-view mirror at Jeffrey Hale. Back at the old farmhouse, as soon as I had opened the car's front door on the passenger's side, my dog had leaped into the seat. I had told him to get into the back, but the Englishman had said hastily, "Let him stay! I wouldn't dream of disputing the point with him."

Now I asked, "Do you come to Italy in the summer to dig for ancient cities, and all that?"

"Not a chance. A foreigner needs the

British Museum or some equally weighty institution behind him to get permission to dig in Italy. But I'm able to study, nevertheless. The museums in Florence and the hill towns around here — Siena and so on — are full of Etruscan and early Roman artifacts."

"In this heat, I should think you would be just as glad not to dig. Is it always like this?"

"Usually not until July and August. But the summers are hot. That's the reason for all the tile and marble floors." Seconds later he said, "That's where I live, up ahead. Your turnoff is about a mile farther on."

I looked at the old farmhouse, almost a duplicate of Althea's, except that it was larger and had several outbuildings in the rear. At the road's edge in front of the house, a stooped old man in a dark suit had just turned away from the mailbox. "Who's that?"

"Domenico Pasquale, my landlord. I rent two rooms from him."

"I see that he's able to afford electricity and telephone." Lines stretched from two roadside poles to the house.

"Yes, he sold off most of his land a few years ago, and at a very good price. Best not to stop and speak to him. We'd never get away. He loves America. For a few years more than fifty years ago he lived in Bronx —"

"*The* Bronx."

"Very well. Although why it shouldn't be also the Manhattan and the Brooklyn, I'll never understand. Anyway, he was a jockey at various tracks around New York. He was also a fan of a baseball team there, the Giants. If you give him a chance, he'll replay the nineteen twenty-three World Series for you in English you can't understand."

"Like, 'then-a he pop-a up to the shorta-stop'?"

He laughed. "About like that. How is it you — Oh, I know. Althea told me. Your mother's parents are Italian."

"Yes. They were both born in Isolotta. I guess that's the reason Althea came here — that, and the fact that Florence is only twenty miles away." We were passing the farmhouse now. The old man had gone inside. "Their name is Rossi. Grandmother was a Rossi even before she married. She and my grandfather are third cousins."

"I'm not surprised. There are about three hundred people in Isolotta. Perhaps half of them are named Rossi. The other half are named Marchetti or Vanezzi, and everyone is at least a third cousin to everyone else."

I drove in silence for a while. Then I asked, "Do you like my sister's paintings?"

After a moment he said, "She's very talented. I have a painting of hers, one she gave me when we were still — seeing each other frequently. A view of the Rafaellos' villa, painted from her window. It's very good."

"But hasn't she changed her style? There's an unfinished painting in her bedroom. It looks very different."

Again he was momentarily silent. Then he said, "Yes, I believe she is trying something new."

"I wish she wouldn't. I've always loved her neo-Impressionist work. And it has sold well."

"Perhaps not recently. Italy has been far from prosperous these past few years."

"And so she changed styles. Are her new pictures selling?"

"I believe so."

"Who handles them? Some gallery in Florence?"

"I really couldn't say."

I looked into the rear-view mirror. His expression was calm and pleasant, and yet

I had the distinct impression that he was lying. Why? If he could tell me more about my sister, why didn't he? Surely he could imagine the anxiety I felt.

Could it be that he even knew where she was now? I thought of how he had called from the foot of the stairs, "Althea? Is that you up there?" But that could have been a trick. Perhaps he had known from the first that it was not my sister beyond that half-opened door.

Well, I thought grimly, I would have other sources of information. There was the Contessa. There were the police. And if necessary, I could try once more to get this evasive Englishman to tell me what he knew.

I asked, "Does the Contessa live alone?"

"Oh, no." He seemed prepared to be quite chatty about the Rafaellos. "Her father-in-law, Michael Rafaello, is at the villa, and her son and daughter. The daughter is engaged to Prince Raspelli."

"A papal prince?"

"No. His title goes back almost to the time of the Medicis. There's your turnoff up ahead, beside that monument. That road will lead you straight to the villa."

"Monument? That thing that looks like a big chunk of marble?"

"Yes. Once a farmhouse stood there. During World War Two, a group of partisans who'd holed up there were wiped out by the Germans. There's a bronze plaque on the monument engraved with the names of the Italians who died."

Seconds later I stopped beside the monument. Irregularly shaped and about the size of a one-car garage, it had a certain rough-hewn impressiveness. Jeffrey Hale got out and took his bicycle down from the rack. Then he said, standing beside me, "Are you sure you won't take my advice?"

"About going home? No. I came here to find Althea, and I won't leave until I do."

His brilliant eyes were unreadable. "Well, good luck."

"Thank you."

Just before I turned left onto the other road, I glanced into the rear-view mirror. Grasping the bike's handlebars, he still stood there looking after me.

4

The road took me over a stone bridge spanning the river, and then led through gently rolling land, past vineyards and neatly kept peach orchards. Soon I could see the villa, halfway up a green hillside, and the long drive, bordered by double rows of cypress, running from the house down to the road. As I ascended the drive, I was grateful for the trees' shade. My wristwatch told me it was almost four o'clock, and yet the air was as hot as it had been at noon.

The drive ended in a loop surrounding a marble fountain ornamented with bronze tritons spouting water. A bed of larkspur and Shasta daisies encircled the fountain. Beyond rose the house with its terra-cotta façade, set with long double windows. On the second floor, each pair of windows opened onto a balcony with a gracefully curving wrought-iron balustrade.

I stopped the car at the foot of the fan-shaped flight of steps. "Wait," I said to Caesar, and climbed to the tall front doors, their panels of etched glass protected by wrought-iron grilles. When I pressed a button set into the wall at the right of the doorway, I heard soft chimes inside the house.

After a moment one half of the door opened. An elderly manservant, clad in black trousers and a black alpaca jacket, bowed slightly and wished me good day in Italian.

I said, also in Italian, "My name is Samantha Develin. May I see the Contessa?"

"Please come in. I will find out if the Contessa is able to see you now."

I stepped into a large entrance hall, rectangular in shape, and with a formal floor of alternate squares of black and white marble. The air here was pleasantly cool. Opposite the doorway, white marble steps led up to a balcony that surrounded the hall on three sides.

"Please sit down," the manservant said, and walked to a wide doorway beyond the left-hand side of the stairs. I sat in a tall armchair with a carved wooden back and looked at the life-sized classical statues — nymphs and goddesses and Greek warriors — standing against the walls of cream-colored stucco. No matter how large the contribution the Contessa's late husband had made to the Church, it was evident that the Rafaellos had not been left impoverished.

Light footsteps. A slender woman in a cool-looking black frock of some light-weight material, her blond hair dressed high and held by little tortoiseshell combs, moved toward me. She was smiling, but I could see the haughtiness Jeffrey Hale had mentioned in her fine-featured face with its high-bridged nose, and in the poise of her small head. She said in excellent though accented English, "Miss Develin? I am Isobel Rafaello."

As I took her narrow outstretched hand, I was aware from the look in her gray eyes that she had expected to meet a quite different sort of person. She hid her surprise better than the Englishman had, but it was there, all right.

"I was about to have tea. Will you join me?"

"That would be lovely."

I followed her back along the side of the staircase and into a vast room, paneled in fruit wood, and set with eighteenth-century French furniture. Here too the floor was marble, but rugs partially covered it. Were they Savonnerie rugs? I had never seen any except in photographs, and so I wasn't sure. Glass doors stretching along one wall of the room showed me the broad marble terrace beyond. A stooped old man, massive bald head bent, was walking slowly beside the balustrade.

"That is my father-in-law," the Contessa said. "I shan't introduce you. He's very old, and finds meeting people a terrible strain."

"Isn't it too hot for him out there?"

"At his age he seems to enjoy the heat." She gestured toward a small settee upholstered in yellow satin. We both sat down. For the first time I became aware of a half-opened door across the room. From beyond it came the murmur of a man's voice and then a girl's soft laughter.

"My daughter Sophia and her fiancé are playing backgammon." The Contessa smiled. "I am sure they will pay no attention to us."

Her smile vanished. "First of all, my dear, I want you to know that I realize how distressed you must be."

"Thank you. And thank you too for notifying the police, and for telephoning me."

She nodded an acknowledgment. "I suppose you intend to see the carabinieri in Isolotta?"

"Yes, as soon as I leave here."

"You will find they have encouraging

47

news. They telephoned me this morning. The Milan police told them that last April they impounded your sister's car because it had been left standing on a street near the railroad station for several days. And so probably, my dear, your sister went off somewhere by train. Perhaps she didn't know that people are not supposed to park on the street indefinitely, although many people do."

My heart bounded with hope. Just as long as she's all right, I thought, just as long as she's all right. But why was she staying away for so many weeks?

The Contessa said, almost as if I had asked the question aloud, "Perhaps she is having a pleasant time, so pleasant that she has extended her stay."

Yes, that could be it.

And then I thought of those two missing letters, the ones I had written to her. I said, "I have written twice to my sister since early last April. She couldn't have received my letters, and yet I did not find them in her mailbox."

She lifted slender hands, palms outward. "Ah, our dreadful Italian mail service! So often overseas letters do not reach us. They are lost in the Rome or Milan post offices."

Perhaps that was what had happened. But it seemed strange that two letters in a row should be lost.

A maid in a calf-length black dress and white apron wheeled a tea cart into the room. Beside the teapot rested a platter of thin sandwiches and another of little frosted cakes. The sight of the food reminded me that I'd had nothing to eat since the coffee-and-croissants breakfast served just before the plane landed that morning.

I also recollected, with dismay, that I hadn't checked to see if there were any tinned foods in that pantry in Althea's kitchen. Well, surely there were at least staples like matches and salt and tinned milk, and so in Isolotta I would buy only enough food to last me until the next day.

Trying not to appear too greedy, I sipped the fragrant jasmine tea the Contessa had poured and ate one of the cucumber and two of the prosciutto sandwiches. Perhaps she saw that I was hungry and wanted me to enjoy the food, because she had turned the conversation to a more pleasant subject, her daughter's approaching marriage.

"The guest list has kept growing and growing. Prince Raspelli has so many relatives who are coming from all over Europe, and hundreds of friends, of course. Because some of them won't be able to arrive until the very day of the wedding, we've had to shift the ceremony from eleven in the morning until four in the afternoon."

Until now, if Jeffrey Hale had not told me otherwise, I would have assumed that Isobel Rafaello came from a long line of self-assured aristocrats. But her tone as she said his name made me realize that she was very impressed by the prospect of Prince Raspelli marrying her daughter. She was even parvenu enough to want to impress me, a little nobody from New York.

"In fact," she went on, "the guest list is so long that we can't hold the reception here. It will be held at a family friend's villa on the other side of Florence."

If her friend's villa was larger than this one, it must be very spacious indeed. She rose and pulled the bell rope beside the black marble fireplace. After perhaps a minute the maid came in and wheeled the tea cart away. The Contessa said, when the servant had gone, "What are your immediate plans?"

"Why, to stay here until I learn where my sister is."

"That I understand. But where will you stay, exactly?"

"At the farmhouse, if that is all right with you."

"Of course you may stay there. But there is the small matter — Oh, one hates to mention these things —"

It dawned on me that she was talking about the rent. "I shall make good those two missing checks, of course."

"Thank you. Perhaps your sister's checks, too, have been temporarily lost in the mail. I know it seems a small matter. But these days one's expenses keep mounting, while one's income goes down and down."

I forbore looking around the luxurious room. Instead I took my book of traveler's checks and a ball-point pen from my shoulder bag. "What is the amount?"

"For the two months?" She named a sum. "And then, of course, there was my long distance phone call."

I signed checks for the total amount. While not an exorbitant sum, it did bite deeply into the funds I had brought with me. Well, no matter. I had my return ticket to Kennedy. And if necessary I could draw on money I had in a New York bank — savings from my salary and from my share of the money left to Althea and me by our parents.

I handed her the checks. Rising, she

placed them on the marble mantelpiece. "Now is there any way in which I can make you more comfortable there at the farmhouse?"

I too stood up. "You might tell me how I can get ice for the icebox."

"You can order it at the grocer's in Isolotta. A member of the grocer's family has an old truck, and he delivers wood and coal in the winter and ice in the —"

She broke off, her face lighting up. She said with an arch smile, "So you two decided not to stay in there forever, after all."

I turned to see that a man and a girl had emerged from that partly opened door. The Contessa said, "Miss Develin, may I present my daughter Sophia? And this is her fiancé, Prince Raspelli."

The tall girl, in light blue jeans and a matching tee shirt, was eighteen or perhaps twenty, and more beautiful than her mother could ever have been. Sun-streaked blond hair, worn shoulder-length, framed an oval face with chiseled features. Her blue eyes were large, wide-spaced, and rather vapid-looking. But with looks like that, who would need intelligence?

The Prince, in white tennis shorts and shirt, was an inch or so shorter than his betrothed, perhaps ten pounds overweight, and, although he appeared not more than thirty, already balding. The fingers with which he raised my hand to his lips were slightly damp. So were his lips. I found that in spite of her beauty and her prospective title of princess, I did not envy Sophia Rafaello.

The Contessa said, "Did you enjoy your game?"

She shrugged. "Giuseppe won. He always does."

The Contessa laughed. "Then you should be glad you are marrying such a clever man."

Sophia was looking at me. "You are Althea Develin's sister?"

"Yes."

I could see that she too was surprised by my appearance, but evidently she was too polite, or perhaps too indifferent, to make any comment. Her mother said, "Shall I ring for tea? Miss Develin and I have had ours."

"It's too hot for tea. Giuseppe and I are going to swim for a while. But it would be nice if you would send some iced sangria down to the pool in about half an hour."

Sophia wished me a good afternoon and her fiancé said he had been enchanted to meet me. Then they went out onto the terrace. The old man, I saw, was now seated in a white wicker chair and apparently asleep, large head sunk on his chest. Sophia and the Prince walked past him and out of my line of vision.

I said, "I really must go." As she moved beside me across the salon, I asked, "How far is Isolotta?"

"Less than two miles. Just keep driving south along the road that brought you here. Soon you'll see Isolotta. It's on top of a hill and surrounded by a wall."

We had just emerged from the salon when the front door opened and a young, dark-haired man, lean and graceful in white duck trousers and a Basque fisherman's shirt of blue and white stripes, came into the entrance hall. "Back so soon?" the Contessa said.

I felt almost incredulous. Could anyone, even an Italian male, be quite that good-looking? He was about six-feet-one-inches tall. Without being in the least effeminate, his features were classically cut, the cheekbones high, the nose aquiline, the mouth mobile and with a full underlip. This man looked the way I had expected Prince Raspelli to look.

"Miss Develin, this is my son Arturo. This is Althea Develin's sister, Arturo."

For a moment his eyes, brown and lustrous under dark brows, held that surprised look I was becoming used to. Then he smiled and bent over my hand. The touch of his lips was brief, warm.

"I am delighted to meet you, Miss Develin. I only regret the unhappy circumstance that has brought you here."

I murmured an acknowledgment.

"That splendid beast out in the Simca must be yours."

"Yes. I hope you didn't —"

"Try to approach him while he was guarding his mistress's car?" He laughed. "Much as I like dogs, I would not be that rash."

I smiled at him, and then turned to his mother. "Thank you for the tea, Contessa."

"You are leaving now?" Arturo Rafaello asked.

"Yes. I want to see the carabinieri in Isolotta."

"I will accompany you to your car."

I said good-bye to the Contessa, and then walked out onto the fan-shaped steps with her son. How old was he? Twenty-six? Perhaps a little older.

He asked as we descended the steps, "How is your Italian?"

"Passable, although probably not as good as when I was a child. My grandparents often spoke Italian to Althea and me."

"Good. The carabinieri here speak no English."

We had reached the Simca. He held out his hand so that Caesar could sniff it. After an indecisive moment the shepherd lolled his tongue in a broad smile.

Arturo said, scratching the dog behind his ears, "I was here when the carabinieri called my mother this morning. I suppose she told you that the Milan police found your sister's car near the railroad station."

"Yes." His mention of the carabinieri reminded me of something I had forgotten to ask his mother. "When the men came to search the farmhouse, apparently they knew that Althea kept the key above the door lintel. Do you have any idea how they knew?"

He looked embarrassed. "Yes. They stopped by here before they went to the farmhouse. I didn't want them to do any damage trying to get in, so I told them where to find the key. You see, once when Althea was to be away, she asked me to go into her house now and then to see if everything was all right."

He was lying, of course. It was not when she was to be "away" that she had given this handsome man ready access to her house. But it was a gallant lie, and I liked him for it.

"Please try not to worry," he said. "I am sure Althea will return soon."

Trying to smile, I nodded.

"Do you plan to stay at the farmhouse?"

"Yes, at least until Althea returns or I have heard from her."

Again he looked faintly embarrassed. "It was because she had received no rent check for two months in a row that my mother realized something might have happened, and that she had better notify the carabinieri. This afternoon, did she —"

"Mention the rent? Yes. I paid it."

"Please try to understand. These days everyone in Italy worries about money."

"There is nothing to understand. Of course your mother was entitled to payment." I smiled at him. "I really must go now."

He walked with me around to the other side of the car and opened the door. When I was seated at the wheel, he said, "Have you ever been to Florence?"

"I've never been out of the United States before."

"Would you meet me at a café there some afternoon or evening soon, so that I might show you around a bit?"

More of his tact. He had not asked to be invited to the farmhouse. Because he did not want me to think that he expected me to fall into bed with him, as Althea probably had, he had suggested that we meet in Florence.

"I would like that very much."

"Good. Since you do not have a telephone, I will send a message to you in a day or two."

He stepped back from the car. We exchanged good-byes, and then I drove around the fountain and descended the drive.

5

When I reached the road, I turned left. As I wound in and out through the gentle hills, some crowned with villas, others with ruined castles dating from some time in Tuscany's long and turbulent past, I wondered if my sister had been in love, even briefly, with the handsome Arturo. Probably not. At least in the past, while she was attending a junior college near Oak Corners, and later on when she worked in New York, it had seemed to be the loser types of whom she was most fond. True, some of the men who drove up to Oak Corners with her for the weekend were rising young lawyers or stockbrokers or advertising executives. But the ones she liked well enough to bring home with her several times were quite different. I recalled a thrice-divorced encyclopedia salesman who talked moodily of how, after eight years in psychoanalysis, he still didn't know what had gone wrong in his marriages. And then there had been a young draftsman and as-yet-unpublished poet, a man so shy that if you spoke to him suddenly, he would give a start and blush.

I turned a curve. Up ahead was a hill whose almost perfect cone shape indicated that it had been formed by an extinct volcano. Atop it was a town, some of its tiled roofs visible above the surrounding walls. Isolotta, undoubtedly. From my grandparents I knew that during Tuscany's fourteenth-century civil wars, a Ghibelline noble had erected a castle on that hill, and sallied forth with his henchmen now and then to harass the Guelphs of Florence. Later the castle had been razed to provide building materials for a village within those walls. Now a few of Isolotta's inhabitants owned small fields at the foot of the hill. But most of them were landless peasants, working in other men's orchards and vineyards, and returning at night to their ancient village. My heart quickened. Now I would see the town where Luigi Rossi and Rosa Rossi grew up, married, and then almost immediately left for America.

The road up the hill was steep. In second gear I passed an old farm truck and a two-wheeled cart drawn by oxen. Evidently now, at around six in the evening, the villagers were returning after what must have been an arduous day's work indeed under the torrid sun. I drove through an entrance tunnel set into the thick wall and emerged into the village.

Telephone and power lines were strung around the big, cobblestoned square. A few trucks and old cars were parked at the curbs. A gas pump stood in front of what was probably the grocery and general store, and a few yards farther on rose a standard lamp with a four-sided green glass shade, probably marking the entrance to the police station. Otherwise, it was as if I had moved back in time several hundred years. The façades of the three-story houses — some of Tuscan ocher brick, some of faded pink stucco, some of dark stone probably once part of the castle — must have looked much the same when Machiavelli was alive. In the center of the square was a large well with at least half a dozen cats stretched out asleep on its coping of dark stone. At the end of the square rose a small church of clay brick, topped by a plain wooden cross. Undoubtedly it was in that church that my grandparents — young, in love, and exhilarated by the prospect of beginning their life together in fabled America — had exchanged vows.

A few people, most of them in dark clothing, the men with dark felt hats and many of the women with shawls over their heads, moved along the sidewalk. The faces they turned to me as I drove toward the police station held not only curiosity but faint suspicion. No doubt few strangers ever came to a village that held no fine buildings or works of art. I stopped the car beside the green-shaded lamp and went through an open doorway.

In the small room beyond, two men, one middle-aged, the other younger, sat behind two tables that apparently served as desks. At sight of me both men got to their feet. Even in this sweltering heat they were in full uniform, with white shoulder straps slanting across their tightly belted tunics. Perhaps regulations forbade their removing their tunics while on duty, or perhaps they were too proud of their status to do so.

I said in Italian, "I'm Samantha Develin, Althea Develin's sister."

Both men bowed, and the older one waved me to a chair opposite him. He said, "The Milan police tell us they found your sister's car last April parked near the railroad station." His accent was different from that of my grandparents and that of Italians I had heard speaking in the Milan airport that morning. I recalled reading somewhere that except for high officials, police forces in the north were made up of

men from Naples and elsewhere in southern Italy.

"I know about my sister's car. Contessa
Rafaello told me. Is there any further
news?" The small room seemed to be
growing hotter. I could feel sweat on my
upper lip.

"Not as yet. After we notified them that
your sister was missing, the Milan police
began questioning ticket sellers at the
Milan railroad station, in the hope that
even after all this time someone might remember a woman of your sister's descrip-
tion. As soon as we hear any news of her,
we will let you know."

"Thank you." I reached into my shoulder bag for a handkerchief and daubed my
upper lip and forehead. "I understand you
searched the farmhouse."

"Not only the house. We searched the
land for a few hundred yards in every direction for any sign of a recent distur-
bance."

My stomach tightened. I knew what he
meant. They had looked for some indication that earth had been dug up.

He asked, "Is there any other way we can
help you?"

"You might tell me where the post office
is, and where I can order ice."

"You will find everything at the grocer's a few doors down. Turn to your left when you go out."

I said good-bye, shook hands with both men, and turned to leave. It was then that I saw why the room had grown so hot. More than a dozen villagers stood just outside the doorway, blocking any stray breeze. Some of the swarthy faces were expressionless. In others hostility was plain.

I moved toward the doorway. The crowd parted. As I turned onto the sidewalk, someone spat out, "Your sister is a *puttana*." I threw a startled look at the speaker. He was a man about the age of my grandfather, wearing not the felt headgear of the other men, but a battered old ship's officer's cap with a visor. His seamed dark face, filled with hate, looked so much like my grandfather's that I was sure they must be cousins.

Trying not to show my shock and humiliation, I moved down the sidewalk, aware that the small crowd was following me. In the window of the grocery hung two dead rabbits by their hind feet, and several strings of tiny plucked birds. I had heard of the Italian custom — repulsive to me, at least — of roasting songbirds on a spit, each so small that it provided not more than two bites.

I went into the long shadowy room, aware that again the hostile little crowd hovered in the doorway. My first astonished hurt had given way to anger. To my left a middle-aged woman, obviously the postmistress, stood behind a grilled window. I said loudly and clearly, "I am Samantha Develin, Althea Develin's sister. Could you tell me if anyone — the mail carrier, say — has returned to you any letters addressed to her?"

"He has not."

"Well, do you recall if any letters were delivered to my sister's since early last April?"

She looked at me with inscrutable dark eyes for a moment and then said, "I think there have been four letters for her in the last two or three months, two from New York and two from Milan. I remember because your sister does not receive much mail." Her tone implied that receiving little mail was another sign of a disreputable character.

"I found no letters at all in her mailbox."

Her only reply was a shrug.

I moved past bushel baskets of oranges, potatoes, green peppers, and squash to where an elderly woman stood at a counter. Behind her rose shelves of canned goods. She looked so much like the post-mistress that I was sure they were mother and daughter.

"My name is —"

"I heard you say your name."

After a moment I went on stiffly, "Could you tell me how much ice my sister orders?"

"In weather like this? Twenty kilos every three days."

"Will you have twenty kilos delivered to me tomorrow?"

"I'll tell my husband."

She stood motionless. I said, "Aren't you going to write my order down?"

"I will remember," she snapped. Too late, I realized that probably she did not know how to write.

"I would like to buy some food."

At my request she placed a half-dozen oranges on the counter, a half-dozen eggs, a box of soda crackers, and cans of milk, coffee, and tuna fish. "Is that all?" When I nodded, she called, "Alicia!"

The postmistress came over and added up my purchases on a pad of paper. "Where is your shopping bag?"

"I have none." Used to American ways, I had assumed the store provided paper bags.

She reached under the counter and brought up a bag of knotted string. "That will be a thousand lire extra," she said, and began to thrust my purchases into the bag.

Carrying my groceries, I turned toward the doorway. Again the small, silent crowd parted for me. A few yards up the street several young men stood looking at the Simca. They were keeping a respectful distance, no doubt because of Caesar's presence in the front seat.

I put my groceries in the back seat and then got behind the wheel. I looked at the people on the sidewalk, their swarthy faces reddened now by the light of the descending sun. Only the young men were smiling, and I did not like the quality of their smiles. Sensing the crowd's hostility and my own distress, Caesar growled. I started the car, made a U-turn over the cobblestones, and drove through the tunnel in the thick northern wall.

As I descended the steep hillside, I recalled Althea's writing to me about her first visit to Isolotta, soon after her arrival in Italy. In her friendly, outgoing way, she undoubtedly had told the villagers that our grandparents had been born there. I could imagine her asking oldsters about Luigi and Rosa Rossi's growing-up years. I could imagine her dandling fat bambinos, fifth or sixth cousins of ours. Perhaps the villagers then had displayed no more than the usual peasant reserve toward any newcomer. But later on —

Oh, why hadn't Althea been restrained by the knowledge that she was in a country where, at least among the peasantry, only the men were allowed sexual license? Did she think that the fact that her grandparents had been born in this part of the world would make the local people more tolerant of her? On the contrary, they must have been doubly outraged that a descendant of fellow villagers would behave in that fashion. Again I thought of the man, hatred in his seamed face beneath the visored cap, who had called Althea a whore.

I realized that my thoughts were verging upon disloyalty to Althea. And that must not be. I thought of the first morning I had moved, dread in my heart, toward the Oak Corners Elementary School. It was my sister, not my shy grandmother, who led me by my small cold hand, and smiled reassurance down at me. Later on, even though she had difficulty with the work assignments she brought home from junior college — Althea never had been much of a scholar — she was always willing to help me with my third-grade arithmetic. She even cut her own classes so that she could be present on Parents' Day at my school, a function that my grandparents, embarrassed by their broken English, were reluctant to attend.

Cruelty was the only real sin, I told myself. And as far as I knew, it was a sin of which Althea never had been guilty.

I drove on through a landscape familiar to me from reproduced paintings I had seen all my life. That hillside over there, its terraced grapevines touched with mauve in the dying sunset, might have served as background for a Fra Angelico painting of the Annunciation. A few minutes later I saw a ruined castle on a hilltop, dark against an apple-green sky. It seemed to me that Leonardo had painted that same castle in the background of his *Adoration of the Magi.*

I made a right-hand turn. Ahead was the farmhouse shared by Jeffrey Hale and the aged Giant fan. On sudden impulse I turned off the road, drove across the bare yard, and stopped the Simca beside a dark blue English Rover. Perhaps if I confronted him, suddenly and unexpectedly, with a question about those missing letters, I might learn something from his reaction.

He must have seen me from an upstairs window, because by the time I had swung the car door open and stepped to the ground, he had emerged from an arched entryway in the building's ocher-brick side and was moving toward me. "Well, how did it go?"

"My visit to the Rafaellos? All right. My sister's car was found near the railroad station in Milan, but otherwise they had no news for me. Neither did the carabinieri in Isolotta." I paused, and then asked, "Didn't you say you've stopped at my sister's house several times since she's been gone?"

"I did."

"The postmistress in Isolotta said that at least four letters had been delivered to my sister's house since early last April. Do you know anything about them?"

He looked startled. Then he said in a cool, deliberate voice, "Aren't the implications of that question rather insulting?"

Too late, I realized that nerve strain had rendered me undiplomatic. Although I felt color in my face, I held my ground. "I thought you might have looked into her mailbox."

"Why should I do that?"

"I don't know. Perhaps to see if the box

had started to overflow. Anyway," I persisted, "those letters have to be someplace."

"And you think perhaps I took them. My dear girl, you are rather a fool. If I had taken the letters, do you think I would admit it?"

I remained silent. I had hoped that his expression, if not his words, would tell me something, but his face was unreadable. He went on, "And if I were the sort of man who steals letters, I might be capable of other things, too. And yet you come here, all by yourself, with your accusations. Don't you see how foolhardy you are?"

I looked at him through the last of the daylight. Were his words a threat, a warning, or only an expression of his annoyance? I said, "Don't you understand? I've got to find my sister."

"Let the police find her. Or let her find herself. She'll come home when she's ready to."

I was silent for a moment, and then burst out, "I think you know something about her, something you're holding back."

After several seconds he answered, "If you think I know where she is, you're completely wrong. Now about those letters.

Don't you realize that anyone around here, passing your sister's place frequently, and seeing no car in the yard and no lights in the windows, would decide that she was away? And don't you realize that the people around here are poor these days, so poor that some of them would rifle a mailbox in the hope of finding an envelope with a check or cash inside?"

I felt both relieved and chagrined. Somehow I had never thought of an ordinary petty thief as the culprit. "Perhaps you're right." I got back into the Simca. "I'm awfully sorry if I was rude."

"You were damned rude." His smile took the sting out of the words. "But then, I know you must be damned upset too." He paused. "Do you still intend to stay here?"

"Yes." A bent figure had appeared in the entryway. Jeffrey Hale's landlord. In no mood to hear a replay of the 1923 World Series, I turned the ignition key. "Goodbye," I said. Making a U-turn, I drove back to the road.

Despite my embarrassment, I was glad I had stopped to talk to Jeffrey Hale. He had made me realize that perhaps there was nothing sinister in the fact of those missing letters. And that, somehow, had made me feel better about my missing sister. Probably he was right. She would come home. Why, even as early as tomorrow night at this time she and I, too busy talking to eat much of the food we had prepared, might be sitting at the old dining table in that room with the red tile floor.

6

It was fully dark by the time I turned into the farmyard. My headlights shone through the doorless openings on the ground floor. Should I drive my car in there? Perhaps Althea had used the old stable area as a garage. Leaving the headlights on, I got out and walked through the left-hand doorway.

Straw on the floor, and in the air, even though decades must have passed since animals were kept here, the faint aromatic smell of cattle dung. In one corner stood a tall metal oil drum. Bending, I tipped the drum so that my headlights shone on its contents. Miscellaneous trash, evidently, including numerous small rags covered with a rainbow of stains where she had wiped her paintbrushes. Why had she allowed so many of those paint rags to accumulate? Surely there was some sort of local dump to which they could have been consigned. It was not like Althea to be careless in such matters. In fact, especially for a creative person, she had always been quite neat.

Like the dead geraniums, this accumulated trash seemed to me an indication that of late some overwhelming preoccupation had made her indifferent to former concerns.

I looked across the stable area to where the glow of the Simca's headlights came more faintly through the other doorway. In the corner over there stood a stack of what looked like old magazines and paperback books. In between, lying on the straw, were a few lengths of rotten-looking wood, probably all that remained of some sort of partition. Best not to drive in here, I decided, until I had made sure that the straw hid no nails or other sharp objects.

I returned to the car, took my groceries from the rear seat, switched off the headlights. Followed by Caesar, I climbed the stairs. After fumbling in my shoulder bag for the big old key, I opened the door. Barely enough light came through the windows to show me the oil lamp on the kitchen table. I took off its tall chimney and, with a match from the box my groping hands found on the shelf above the kitchen sink, lit the wick. Thanks to an attached reflector, the lamp's glow was almost as bright as that of a hundred-watt bulb.

As I should have done before I went grocery shopping, I checked the supplies Althea had left. In the bread box on the sinkboard, a quarter of a loaf of long Italian bread, now rock-hard. In the pantry cupboard, a canned ham, several cans of soup, and lots of staples — salt, cubed sugar, vinegar, bottled olive oil, and many spices. Then, crouching, I opened the icebox door.

Dismayed, and with nostrils quivering, I surveyed its interior. About half a ham, now covered with greenish mold. A tin of opened, and very sour, condensed milk. Melted butter or margarine that had overflowed its small dish to lie caked on the box's enamel floor. A bunch of shriveled carrots.

The hopefulness I had felt only a few minutes ago vanished. If she had planned to be away for any length of time, surely Althea would have thrown this food out or, more likely, given it to someone. She would not have left it to decay malodorously in the heat.

I cleaned out the contents of the box onto one of a stack of newspapers I found beneath the sink, and then deposited the newspaper, tightly rolled, in the garbage can. I heated a pan of water on the stove, added powdered soap from a cardboard container on the windowsill near the sink, and scrubbed out the icebox.

That task, plus my renewed anxiety, left me with little appetite. Nevertheless I managed to eat a meager meal of crackers and most of the small can of tuna, with an orange for dessert. I gave the rest of the tuna to Caesar. Usually I fed him only once a day, but he loved tuna, and I felt a special treat might make him feel more at home in this strange place.

Afterwards I went into the bedroom, lit the lamp on the nightstand, and carried it over to the little desk. I opened the shallow drawer and began to lay its contents on the desk top. A box of plain white notepaper with matching envelopes. Several ball-point pens. A packet of letters in Italian, written by our grandmother over the years. Two much thicker packets of letters from me, the first mailed seven years ago, the last one the previous February. No other letters of any kind. But then, Althea had never been a letter-saver. I felt touched that she kept our grandmother's letters and my own.

Apparently the drawer was empty now. No, there was something else, something whose thin rectangular shape was barely discernible beneath the plain white paper lining the drawer. I reached beneath the living and drew out a sheet of drawing paper.

It bore a charcoal sketch of a smiling female statue — made of some sort of metal, to judge by the highlights. She wore an elaborately pleated gown. In her right hand she held what might have been a leafy branch, and in her left something that might have been a spindle. Whatever it was, the end of it obviously had been broken off. Was the figure Greek? Early Roman? I did not think so. There was something semi-Oriental in the rigidly waved coiffure ending in shoulder-length curls, and the wide-spaced, almond-shaped eyes.

Those light, feathered charcoal strokes were so like those of other sketches of Althea's that I was sure she had made the drawing. As for the figure itself, it probably was part of a museum collection in Florence or Siena. But it seemed strange that she had drawn it, since as far as I knew she had never had much interest in sculpture. And why had she placed it beneath the drawer lining? Merely to keep it from curling, or to hide it?

As I went on looking at that figure, I found I did not like it. There was something almost frightening about that smile. Like the smile of the Mona Lisa, it was enigmatic, detached, inhuman, the smile of a witch in command of dark and mysterious forces.

Had Althea shown this drawing to Jeffrey Hale? Perhaps. In any case the Englishman, an archaeologist particularly interested in this part of Italy, would be able to identify the figure for me.

I placed the sketch back beneath the lining paper, and restored the drawer's other contents. Then, suddenly aware of the long day's accumulated fatigue, I moved to the bed and turned down the spread, the two light blankets, and the top sheet. Obviously the linen had not been slept on since it last was laundered. The pillowcase and both sheets were as smooth as if they had been ironed only that morning. I turned and went into the bathroom and lifted the wicker hamper's lid. Yes, right on top were rumpled sheets and a pillowcase. Not long before she left, obviously, she had changed the bed linen.

But why, if she knew that she was to be away for many weeks? Surely the more normal procedure would have been to strip the bed, so that it would air out during her absence. Again, as when I stood at the kitchen window early that afternoon, and when I looked about an hour ago at the food left in the icebox, I felt a cold conviction that Althea's long absence had not been premeditated. What had happened in this isolated place nearly three months ago to make her suddenly flee from it?

If she had fled.

That grove of olive trees just east of the terrace. They had searched the ground around the house thoroughly, the carabinieri had said. Nevertheless, tomorrow I too would search.

I stood motionless in the lamplight for a moment, aware that the cold anxiety I felt was not just for Althea but for myself as well. Then I went into the shadowy kitchen to make sure that I had turned that big old key in the lock. I had.

Go to bed, I told myself. That heavy old door was locked. Caesar would give the alarm if anyone set even one foot on the stairs. And if someone did manage to get in, Caesar would tear him to pieces.

I went into the bedroom, undressed, and put on a short blue cotton nightgown I took from my suitcase. Then I slipped between those freshly laundered sheets, lifted the lamp chimney, and blew out the flame. Aware of the smell of the extinguished wick lingering in the darkness, I slid deeper into the bed.

A jet flew over, probably a Rome-bound plane from Milan. In the distance, too far away to elicit even a token growl from Caesar, a dog barked for perhaps half a minute.

After that, silence broken only by the shepherd's even breathing as he lay beside the bed. Soon I was asleep.

Caesar's thunderous barks awoke me from a dream in which I watched my grandfather burn red and brown autumn leaves in the gutter in front of our Oak Corners house. I sat up in bed in the pitch-darkness, confused, not even knowing where I was. I could still smell those burning leaves.

Not leaves. Something else burning.

I swung out of bed, groped wildly on the nightstand for the box of matches I had left there, couldn't find it. That flashlight. Where had I seen a flashlight? Oh, yes, in the top bureau drawer. I moved across the room, overturning a straight chair in the pitch-blackness, and jerked the upper drawer open. My groping hand found the metal cylinder. If the battery was dead —

It was not. As I ran into the kitchen, with the furiously barking dog racing back and forth between me and the front door, the flashlight's powerful beam shone on the fire extinguisher on the wall near the stove. I moved to the door, unlocked it, and then, before plunging down the stairs, recrossed the kitchen to snatch down the extinguisher.

The acrid smell of smoke was heavier on the staircase. How had my dreaming self confused that smell with the fragrance of burning leaves? At the foot of the stairs I turned left and ran around the corner of the house to the bare front yard.

Silvery in the starlight, smoke poured out the doorless openings on the ground floor. Cutting through the smother, the flashlight's beam showed me that the tall metal container filled with paint-stained rags and other trash was afire. Flames already licked at the overhead beams.

I had to take a few precious seconds to read the directions on the side of the fire extinguisher. Then, after laying the flashlight on the ground, its beam directed toward the stable, I took off the extinguisher's cap, put my finger on the plunger, and moved toward the doorway. Caesar gave a tremendous bark and then, gathering up a mouthful of my nightgown, tried to pull me back. At my sharp order he let go and retreated, whimpering. I plunged through the opening and, coughing and teary-eyed, directed the extinguisher's jet of powder at the flames. Trying to breathe as shallowly as possible, I kept my finger on the plunger for perhaps two minutes. When I could no longer see any flames, I retreated to the yard and leaned against the side of the Simca, with Caesar pressed close against my bare leg. I stayed there, coughing, until most of the smoke had cleared away from the stable.

Suddenly aware that I was barefoot and I might encounter nails or broken glass on that straw-strewn dirt floor, I picked up the flashlight, ran upstairs, took soft-soled slippers from beneath the bed, and put them on. Swiftly I belted my terry-cloth robe around me. Trailed by Caesar, I returned to the yard and laid the flashlight on the ground.

The fire seemed to be out, but the mess inside the container still steamed, and I did not want to take the chance of leaving it there. The oil drum, I found, was still far too hot for me to handle with bare hands. I looked about me and saw an old rake with wooden teeth propped against the stable's rear wall. Using the rake, I tipped the oil drum onto its side and rolled it, spewing charred cloth and other blackened trash, until it was about twenty feet beyond the stable opening. I picked up the flashlight and directed its beam onto my watch. Almost three-thirty. Then once more I leaned against the side of the car, my heart still racing.

Had the fire started through spontaneous combustion? It certainly might have. I recalled thinking as soon as I saw those paint-stained rags that it had been dangerously careless of Althea to leave them there. But it seemed a coincidence indeed that the drum's contents should have burst into flames only hours after I had moved into the farmhouse.

I thought of someone moving across the yard through the darkness, setting the drum's contents afire, and then slipping away, aware that the house's ancient timbers — the stable's overhead beams, the underflooring and beams upstairs, and the wooden stairs themselves — would burn like so much tinder once they caught. True, if the arsonist knew of Caesar's presence, he or she must also have known that the dog would probably arouse me in time to escape the fire. But he or she must also have calculated that even if I did not die, the experience would leave me so shattered that I would flee back to New York.

Who could have wanted me to do that? The answer seemed obvious: someone who was determined that I should not find out what had happened to Althea. It could have been anyone in this vicinity, I realized, just as it could have been anyone who took those letters from the mailbox. On the other hand, it might have been someone I had met the afternoon before. Certainly it could have been my English neighbor a few miles down the road. It could have been one of the Rafaellos, even though that seemed unlikely since they were the ones who had summoned me here. Or someone could have slipped out of that walled town and driven through the moonless dark to this lonely farmhouse.

The darkness. It stretched all around me. Did it conceal a watcher, someone in the grove of olive trees east of the terrace, or crouched among the espaliered grapevines across the road? I did not think so. If someone had set that fire, he was miles away from here by now. I was sure of it, because even though I did not know my enemy's identity — if indeed I had an enemy — I knew something about him. He did not want to risk apprehension for his criminal act. In fact, he did not want anyone to know that it was a criminal act that had brought about my death or sent me fleeing from the country. Otherwise he would not have set that fire. He would have taken the more dangerous but surer way — shot the lock off that heavy door upstairs, tried to put a bullet through Caesar before the leaping dog could fasten fangs in his throat, and then shot me. With the nearest house three miles away, there would have been no one to hear the shots, or Caesar's barking, or my screams.

Yes, plainly he wanted to use indirect, if less certain, means of getting me out of the way. But later on, if he became desperate —

For a moment I had an almost irresistible impulse to go upstairs, pack my bag, and start driving back to the Milan airport. But no, I could not go home until I had found my sister, whether alive or dead.

For the first time, standing there in the pre-dawn chill, I forced myself to face squarely the thought that my lovely and generous sister might have been killed. If she had been, I resolved, with bitter grief and rage crowding my throat, I would find out how and why she died.

Sometime today I would start searching the overgrown land around this house. But it was not the first thing I would do. The first thing, I decided grimly, would be to drive into Florence and, as soon as the shops were open, buy a gun.

I went upstairs. The smell of smoke still lingered there. Because I knew there was no chance I would get back to sleep, I dressed and sat down to wait for daylight.

7

On the autostrada an overturned tractor-trailer truck held up traffic for almost an hour. Thus it was close to noon when, following the directions given me by a dapper policeman back on Florence's busy Via Calzaioli, I entered a small sporting goods store on a narrow side street. When I had exchanged good mornings with the middle-aged man behind the counter, I said, "I would like to buy a small gun, perhaps a revolver."

"Certainly. May I see your permit?"

"Permit?"

"Yes, from the police department. You must have one before I can sell you a gun."

I said, dismayed, "How do I —"

"You must go to the police headquarters on Via Cavour. You'll find it a few yards north of the Duomo."

The Duomo, I knew, was the cathedral with its enormous dome and its almost festive façade of pink, white, and green marble. I had hurried past it, too grim and worried to feel more than a faint temptation to linger. "How long does it take to get a permit?"

"If one is a foreigner?" He shrugged. "Surely weeks, if one is able to obtain a permit at all."

Weighted with disappointment, I went out to the sidewalk. It was a mere tilted rim, scarcely eighteen inches wide, skirting the solid row of stone building fronts. The day was much cooler than the day before, but even so the air here in this narrow winding street was uncomfortably warm. Vespas and taxis and private cars sped past, honking their horns and missing by inches any pedestrian who, giving way to another pedestrian on that narrow sidewalk, moved off the curb into the street. When I stepped off to make room for an elderly woman coming toward me, a Vespa sped past so close that I could feel the heat of its exhaust. I reflected that if Florence had more famous paintings and statues than any city of its size in the world, it probably also had the most crowded accident wards.

I had just turned onto Via Calzaioli when I saw Arturo Rafaello moving toward me. Today he did not wear white ducks and a striped jersey. Instead he was every inch the well-dressed businessman — dark suit of Italian stubbed silk, white shirt, and striped tie. At sight of me he smiled and quickened his pace.

"Good afternoon, Miss Develin. Are you sight-seeing?"

"No, I —" I broke off, somehow embarrassed to tell this handsome young Italian that I had tried to buy a gun.

His smile vanished. "Are you in some difficulty?"

"Well, something rather frightening did happen last night."

"Would you like to tell me about it over lunch? I was going to my favorite restaurant near the Strozzi Palace. But perhaps you would prefer an outdoor café, like the one in the Piazza della República."

"I would like that very much."

As we moved down the sidewalk through the crowd of smartly dressed Florentines, I asked, "What are you doing in Florence? I should think you would much prefer your villa."

"But I work here in the city! I was at home yesterday only because it was a local holiday, the Feast of St. Peter and St. Paul."

"What sort of work?"

"I am a banker. In fact, I am a vice-president in charge of loans."

I blurted out, before I could stop myself, "At your age?"

He smiled. "An uncle of mine owns this particular bank. That helps."

"I imagine it does." I also felt that his loan department must do a land-office business, especially among the women of Florence.

When we reached the Piazza della República, we sat down at an awning-shaded table in the outdoor café at one edge of the vast square. After the waiter had taken our order, Arturo said, "Would you like to tell me what happened last night?"

I told him. "I realize," I finished, "that the fire could have started all by itself."

"Yes, and it probably did. Still, it must have been a highly unpleasant experience."

"It was. I keep thinking that if Caesar's barking hadn't awakened me —"

"Oh, yes, that magnificent dog of yours. Where is he now?"

"I left him at the farmhouse. I don't like to leave him shut up, but neither do I like leaving him in a parked car for hours, not in warm weather."

I fell silent, thinking of how that morning I had hesitated for perhaps a minute before getting into the Simca. It had stood outside the house all night, both before and after the fire. If someone had wired it, so that when I stepped on the starter — Then I told myself not to be absurd. In the pre-dawn darkness I had decided that my enemy, if I had one, wanted to make it appear that I had suffered an accident. And death in a car wired to explode could never pass as that. I had gotten into the Simca and, except for the traffic tie-up, driven without incident to Florence and left the car in a parking lot on the other side of the Ponte Vecchio.

Arturo said, "Have you notified the carabinieri in Isolotta about the fire?"

"Not yet." I shrank from the thought of paying another visit to that hilltop village.

"Perhaps you should. It might make you feel less nervous about staying at the farmhouse alone — that is, if you do feel nervous."

"I do, a little."

"If my mother were not so busy with arrangements for my sister's wedding, I would suggest to her that she ask you to stay —"

"Oh, no! I couldn't accept such an invitation."

Nor did I want to go to a hotel in Florence. In the first place, I had heard Florence hotels were very expensive during the summer. In the second and even more important place, I wanted to be there at the farm if Althea returned, or if some letter arrived with a clue as to how I might find her.

I said, "No, I'll stay at the farmhouse. But I would feel better if I had some protection besides my dog."

"Do you mean a gun?" He seemed to find the idea neither startling nor foolish.

"Yes."

He nodded. "It might be well to have one. I carry a gun in the glove compartment of my car at all times. Far too many Italian businessmen have been forced to the side of the road lately and kidnapped."

"Yes, I've read about that." I paused, and then said, "I had tried to buy a gun in a shop minutes before I saw you."

He smiled. "And the shopkeeper told you you must have a police permit."

I nodded. "And that it will take weeks to get the permit, if I can get it at all."

"No, it won't, not in your case. When we have finished lunch, we will walk to police headquarters — it's in a Medici palace, by the way — and get your permit." As I looked at him, grateful and impressed, he added lightly, "What is the use of having influence, if you do not use it?"

"But will you have time? If you have to get back to the bank —"

"The bank won't reopen until three-thirty. In Florence, almost everything except the restaurants closes down for at least two hours in midday."

Our food came then. As we ate asparagus and filet of sole and sipped a chilled white wine — a local one, Arturo said — I was aware of the tourists streaming past the café tables, speaking to each other in German, or American-accented English, or other languages I could not identify. Sunburned, camera-festooned, both sexes wearing bright shirts which hung loose over the waistbands of pants or shorts, they looked rumpled and ungainly here among the elegant Florentines.

Arturo said, looking at the sidewalk crowd, "I'm often surprised that even our Leonardos and Michelangelos are enough to bring them here."

"Surprised?"

"Yes. I am sure that Florence is one of the least livable cities in the world. It is as noisy as Bombay, and its traffic is more deadly. In late July and August it is so hot that all the windows are closed and shuttered early in the morning, and remain that way until after sunset. A dreadful place!"

I sensed that he didn't mean a word of it. He was like the legendary Chinese gentleman, hiding his pride in his family and his richly furnished house by references to his "miserable children," and his "unworthy dwelling."

I said, "And you love every sun-baked stone in Florence."

His smile flashed. "Of course. I am a Florentine."

When our lunch was finished, we walked a few hundred yards — past the cathedral and Giotto's airy and graceful bell tower, past the tourists gathered before the Baptistry's great bronze doors — to what must be the most sumptuously housed police station in the world. We moved through the archway of the stone palace built for the first Medici ruler. In the roofed courtyard beyond, Arturo said, "The police offices are here on the ground floor. Why don't you go up those stairs to what was once the Medicis' private chapel? I will come up and get you when your gun permit is ready."

I climbed broad marble stairs to a landing. A sign there pointed to a much shorter flight of stairs at my left. I climbed them and found myself in a tiny jewel box of a room, with a coffered ceiling of dark blue ornamented with gilt stars. Along the walls a painted procession of figures — some on foot, some mounted on richly caparisoned horses — streamed through a magical landscape of marble crags, twisted trees of a species I did not recognize, and bushes bearing red blossoms. The attendant, a woman, told me that the fresco represented the Journey of the Magi, with members of the Medici family depicted as the three kings.

I was still noticing details of that colorful procession — a lone woman, thin and middle-aged, among a crowd of men, and a stag bouncing away over those crags from a pursuing greyhound — when Arturo joined me. My permit was ready.

In a big private office on the ground floor, I showed my passport to an extremely polite official and signed the form, its blank spaces already filled in, which would permit me to buy a gun.

"Signor Rafaello tells me," the man behind the desk said, "that there was a fire of perhaps suspicious origin at the farmhouse where you are staying. That area is beyond our jurisdiction, but if you would care to telephone the carabinieri in

Isolotta, please use our phone."

"Thank you." I felt relieved that I would not have to face those hostile villagers again. The polite policeman dialed the number and then handed the phone to me.

I recognized the voice at the other end of the line as that of the elder of the Isolotta carabinieri. Yes, he assured me, he or his colleague would come to the farmhouse late that afternoon.

When I had hung up, I again thanked the police official for the permit. Then Arturo and I left. In the courtyard he said, "And now to buy that gun."

A few minutes later I stood beside him in the gun shop, gingerly handling a small revolver. Instructed by both Arturo and the shop owner, I learned how to load and unload the weapon, and snap the safety on and off. When we were again out on the narrow sidewalk, with the gun weighting my shoulder bag, Arturo glanced at his watch and said, "I still have half an hour. Is there any other way I can help?"

"You might tell me a good place to shop for groceries."

"There is a large market near here. I will tell you how to get there once we have reached the corner."

Moving single file, we made our way

back over that perilous sidewalk to Via Calzaioli. "Turn right at the next street. You will find a market a few doors down. You might ask them if they deliver groceries. Some Florence markets do deliver out in the country for an extra charge."

"Thank you." I hesitated, and then said, "There's one more thing. Do you know what gallery in Florence carries my sister's paintings? Not that I have time to go there today. But if I know where it is —"

He said after a moment, "No, I don't know where her gallery is located."

"Well, I'll find out somehow. And I really don't know how to thank you for all you've done for me today."

"Perhaps you might thank me by having dinner with me tomorrow night. I could call for you about seven, and we could drive up to the outdoor café in the Piazzale Michelangelo. The view of the city from there is quite remarkable."

"I would enjoy that very much."

We said good-bye then, and I hurried to the market, where I bought bread and a large can of minestrone for my dinner that night, and put my purchases in the string shopping bag I had carried folded up in my shoulder bag. I also ordered butter, milk, and a number of other items to be delivered to the farmhouse the next day. By then, if those dour-looking women in the Isolotta store kept their word, I would have twenty kilos of ice.

As for myself, I had begun to feel remarkably undour. Strange, I reflected, how two-and-a-half hours spent with a handsome man could change your whole outlook. I felt now that the contents of that oil drum had burst spontaneously into flame, as an accumulation of oil- or paint-soaked cloths often do. I also had swung back to feeling that I would see Althea soon. She had gone on a trip, that was all, perhaps with some new man. I pictured her basking on the shore of a Swiss lake beside that unknown man, or sitting with him on a hotel terrace in Marrakech. As for the food she had left in the icebox, perhaps that, like the dead geraniums, was merely an indication that in some ways she *had* changed. But her having fallen into careless habits was scarcely proof that something disastrous had happened to her.

Carrying the string bag, I hurried toward the bridge. To my left I could see a large square, and at its far edge an ancient stone building topped by a tall, crenellated tower. From photographs I had seen I knew that it must be the Palazzo Vecchio with its outdoor gallery displaying some of the world's most famous statues. I resisted the urge to cross the street for a closer look. After all, if the carabinieri were kind enough to drive to the farm to investigate my "suspicious fire," I ought to be there to greet them.

And then I did stop, arrested by the sight of a gift shop window. It held cheap souvenirs — painted ash trays, salt cellars of some dubious-looking silvery metal, cigarette boxes of gilded wood. And standing against the low partition at the window's rear was a painting of Giotto's Tower in a pale wooden frame. In technique, in size and shape of the canvas, and in every other respect it looked like a completed version of that unfinished painting on the easel back at the farmhouse. I leaned closer. Yes, the canvas was signed A. E. Develin. The "E" was for Elaine.

Feeling numb, I went inside. A plump woman with hennaed hair came around from behind a counter holding perfume atomizers. I said, "I noticed that painting in your window. Do you have others by the same artist?"

"As it happens, we do have two others, and at the same price, fifteen thousand lire each."

Fifteen thousand lire. About twenty-five dollars. "She is tremendously talented," the woman went on. "At that price her pictures are the best bargain you'll find in Florence."

"Could I see the others?"

"Of course, of course. They are still unframed, but I could have them framed by tomorrow. Or I'll reduce the price three thousand lire if you would rather have them framed by someone else." She stepped briskly across the room to where, on the floor, a double row of canvases leaned against the wall, only their backs visible to the viewer. "I think hers are the first two."

She bent, picked up the outermost canvas of each row, and turned their faces toward me. "Yes, I was right."

In silence I looked at the paintings, one of the Duomo, the other of the Ponte Vecchio, the ancient bridge I had crossed that morning.

"If you like her work, you would be wise to take all three of them. She paints very little."

Still in silence, I stepped past her. I turned what were now the outermost of the canvases in both rows around. One was of the Duomo, the other of the Ponte

Vecchio. I replaced them, faces turned inward.

When I straightened, I found the woman looking at me, her face cold and defiant. "All right! Those pictures are still a bargain. Where else can you find a genuine oil painting for that price? And your friends back in America won't know there are a lot just like it."

I said, "How long has she been painting such pictures?"

The woman shrugged. "I've been handling them for almost two years now. Perhaps other shops were stocking them even earlier. I know her work is on sale at perhaps a dozen places in Florence." Her gaze sharpened. "Do you know her?"

"Yes. She used to paint very differently. Sometimes her pictures sold for almost a thousand dollars."

The woman raised thin eyebrows. "Really? And how many of those paintings did she do in a year? How many did she *sell* the last few years? Not many. She told me that herself." When I remained silent, she rushed on, "She can do one of these paintings in an hour. I sold almost two hundred of them last summer. Her work may sell even better in some of the other shops. Don't you Americans have some sort of saying about Woolworth making more money than Tiffany?"

When I still did not answer, she said, "Well, do you want to buy a painting or don't you?"

I did not. Nevertheless, I said, "I'll take one of the Ponte Vecchios."

In silence, and with expert swiftness, she wrapped the canvas in green paper. When I had paid her, she said, "If you see Miss Develin, tell her that I'm still waiting for more Giotto's Towers. They outsell the other two combined."

Carrying the picture and my shopping bag, I left the store and crossed the Ponte Vecchio, blind now to the ware displayed by goldsmiths and silversmiths whose stalls lined both sides of the ancient span. Why was Althea betraying her talent? Surely she didn't need money that badly. True, she used to count it a good year if she sold seven or eight paintings. But she also had income from her share of the money left us in our parents' wills. Why had she taken to painting lifeless pictures as mechanically — and no doubt with as little enjoyment — as if she worked on an assembly line?

One thing I was almost certain of. Both Jeffrey and Arturo knew the sort of places where my sister's work was on sale these days. Neither of them had wanted to tell me.

In the parking lot at the other end of the bridge, I put my shopping bag and Althea's painting in the front seat, and got behind the wheel.

8

As I neared the farmhouse, I saw with surprise that the oil drum, which I had left lying on its side in the yard, now stood upright at the road's edge. When I drove into the yard, my surprise turned to indignation. Some officious person had taken it upon himself to gather up the oil drum's strewn and blackened contents.

Had it been Jeffrey Hale? I was sure of it. I got out of the car and walked back to the oil drum. Empty. When the carabinieri arrived, I would have no evidence to show them, except for the slightly scorched overhead beams in the stable, that there had even been a fire.

Inwardly fuming, I carried my groceries and Althea's painting up the stairs. Beyond the heavy door Caesar had set up a joyous barking. I took out the key, opened the door, and set my burdens upon the table. When Caesar felt he had given me a sufficiently demonstrative welcome, he rushed outside. I began to put away my purchases.

I had just placed the little gun in the

nightstand beside my bed when Caesar started barking again. Now the sound held that belligerence with which he met invaders of any premises he considered under his protection. Had the carabinieri arrived? Quickly I went down the stairs.

A dark blue Rover, with Jeffrey behind the wheel, stood near the Simca. As I approached, he said, "Call off your monster, will you?"

I turned to the bristling shepherd. "It's all right. Quiet now."

Caesar obeyed. Sliding out of the car, Jeffrey said, "Those old paint cloths caught fire, didn't they?"

"Yes," I said coldly.

"Damn careless of Althea to have left them there. Once or twice when I dropped by to see if she'd come back, I thought of putting the oil drum out onto the road. Then I realized there might be some reason she didn't want the drum emptied, so I left it there."

"But today you did gather up all that burned stuff, didn't you?"

"Yes. A truck drives by once a week and takes whatever is left at the roadside to the district dump. I was sure you didn't know that, and so would miss the collection."

"Very neighborly of you."

He shot me a quizzical look. "Why that tone?"

"Because I have asked the carabinieri here! I'm not at all sure that trash caught fire all by itself. Maybe they wouldn't have been able to tell whether or not it had. But at least they would have had something to judge by if you hadn't had all the evidence carted off."

He said after a moment, "Sorry. I was just trying to be helpful."

Perhaps that was the case. I said grudgingly, "Well, I suppose it doesn't matter too much."

Caesar had been sniffing the Englishman's shoes. Now he began to wave his plumed tail. Jeffrey said, patting the massive head, "At least your dog likes me. And dogs are infallible judges of character, you know."

"On the contrary, I think dogs are lousy judges of character. Remember that repulsive Bill Sykes in *Oliver Twist*? That dog he kept kicking around simply adored him."

Jeffrey's brilliant blue eyes studied me. "You really are annoyed, aren't you?"

"It's just that you've made a fool of me! Here I notify the carabinieri —"

I broke off. A small car of a make I did not recognize was approaching along the road. It turned into the yard and stopped. As Jeffrey and I approached it, the younger of the carabinieri got out and saluted us. "Good day, signorina, signore. I have been told you wished me to investigate a fire of perhaps suspicious origin."

"I'm afraid —" I began, and then stopped.

"Thanks to me," Jeffrey said, "there is little to inspect. I drove by this morning during Miss Develin's absence and saw burned debris littering the yard, as well as the oil drum in which Miss Develin's sister deposits paint-soaked rags. I raked up the mess, dumped it into the drum, and put the drum beside the road to be emptied." He paused. "The young lady has not indicated as yet whether or not she intends to charge me with destruction of evidence."

The carabiniere looked startled, and then smiled. "Let us hope it does not come to that. You are Signore Hale, are you not, the professor who each summer shares Domenico Pasquale's house?"

"I am."

They were smiling at each other in man-to-man fashion. I got the message. The Englishman was a learned man and a well-established figure in the district, whereas I was not only a newcomer, but the sister of a woman whose conduct had been a public scandal.

The carabiniere turned to me. "Then is there any way I can serve you, signorina?"

My voice was stiff. "There is still the oil drum itself, and the beams in the stable."

The three of us walked back to the stable. "Ah, yes," the carabiniere said, looking upward, "slightly scorched. But that would be the case whether or not the fire's origin was spontaneous."

"Brilliant!" I wanted to say, but contented myself with "Obviously."

We walked out to the road. The carabiniere leaned over the oil drum and sniffed. "Turpentine."

"Turpentine!" I cried. By adding turpentine, an arsonist could have made sure that the fire he kindled would burn swiftly and fiercely.

"Of course," Jeffrey Hale said. "Those paint-stained cloths must have reeked of turpentine. Painters use a turpentine solution to clean their brushes."

"Exactly," the carabiniere said. "I was just about to remind the signorina of that."

Again they exchanged that man-to-man smile. Jaws clamped, I watched them. Then the carabiniere turned to me. "Did you hear anything suspicious during the night? A car driving up or driving away, or anything else that might have indicated the presence of an intruder?"

I had to admit that I had not.

"Then unless there is something else I can do for you, signorina —"

"There isn't." I summoned up a smile. "Thank you for coming."

When the carabinieri had left us, Jeffrey said, "I suppose you want me to clear off too."

"No," I said crisply. "As a matter of fact, I want to talk to you. Shall we go around to the terrace?"

Today was cool enough that we could sit on the wrought-iron chairs drawn up to the table. I said, "I drove to Florence this morning."

"To see the sights?"

"Primarily to buy a gun."

"A gun!" He looked at me, frowning. "You do have the wind up over that fire, don't you?"

"If you mean, do I think that someone may have set it, I certainly do."

"Now why would anyone do that?"

"Perhaps not to kill me. Just to frighten me away, so that I would stop asking questions about my sister."

His face was unreadable now. "Well, if

you insist upon staying alone here, perhaps it is just as well that you have a gun. Do you know how to handle it?"

"Yes. The shopkeeper and Arturo showed me."

"Arturo who?"

"Rafaello."

"Oh, that one. You met him yesterday?"

"Yes. His mother introduced us. And today we ran into each other in Florence and had lunch together. Afterwards he talked the police into issuing me a gun permit."

"Are you going to see him again? Or is that none of my business?"

"Yes, that is none of your business, and yes, I'm going to see him again. He's taking me to dinner tomorrow night."

Again he frowned. "Look here, Samantha. I know he's rich and good-looking and loaded with Latin charm. But a man like that can be poison."

"If a woman said that about another woman, it would be called cattiness. What do you men call it when you say such things?"

He smiled. "You're still angry about that oil drum, aren't you?" His smile vanished. "Nevertheless, I'm telling you. When Arturo marries, the girl will be an Italian, and of his own class, or better, if he can manage it. The Rafaellos are a family on their way up. Look at his sister, marrying into the old aristocracy. He'll wine and dine a girl like you, and flatter you, and do his best to seduce you, but what he'll never do is take you seriously."

"What makes you so sure I want to be taken seriously?"

"I don't know. I'm just sure you're that kind."

He was right about that. Even if I tried to, I could never achieve Althea's casual attitude about men, nor did I want them to regard me lightly. But I could not say that without appearing to take a holier-than-she view of my own sister.

He said, "Didn't you have something else you wanted to talk about?"

"Yes, Althea's pictures." I looked at him squarely. "Today I was in a souvenir shop that sells them — or rather, one of the shops."

He remained silent.

"You knew, didn't you, that she's been turning out the same pictures over and over again, like — like so many sausages. And yet you didn't tell me. Why?"

"I'm sure you know. It was sheer cowardice. I could tell you were very proud of your sister, and I knew you'd be distressed to learn she had turned to hack work."

"Why did she?"

"I suppose because she makes more money that way."

"But why does she want money so much? She's never spent a great deal on clothes. Her rent here is cheap. She has income from a trust fund, and surely some of her pictures were selling — her serious pictures, I mean. And so *why?*"

His only answer was a shrug. I said after a long moment, "There is something I would like to show you, if you can spare a few more minutes."

"I can spare as many as you like."

"Then I'll be right back."

I went upstairs. Perhaps because he had taken a liking to the Englishman, or perhaps to keep an eye on him, Caesar remained on the terrace. When I came down again, I was carrying that strange sketch I had found in Althea's desk. I handed it to him.

As he studied it, I saw growing amazement in his face. "Where did you get this?"

I told him. "I'm sure Althea drew it. But what is it?"

"An Etruscan goddess. The symbolic objects in her hands tell you she is a goddess.

Her features, and the style of her hairdress and garment, tell you that she is Etruscan.

"The Etruscans were a mysterious people, you know," he went on, gathering excitement in his voice. "They left no literature — just a few inscriptions on tombs and monuments that so far have resisted full translation — so that most of the little we know about them comes from what the Romans wrote long after Rome had conquered Tuscany. But one thing is certain from the style of their art, and from the clothing and facial features of their statues. They must have come to Italy about a thousand years before Christ from somewhere in what we now call the Middle East — Mesopotamia, or Libya, or Egypt."

He fell silent for a moment, and then said, "The truly amazing thing about this sketch is that it depicts no known work of Etruscan art."

I said after an incredulous moment, "Now how can you possibly —"

"Because I know every Etruscan artifact discovered so far. I've seen everything in the museums throughout Italy, and in the British Museum, and the Metropolitan in New York. And I've seen photographs of every other Etruscan object in museums around the world."

I could not have said why, but his words, like the strange smile on the face in that sketch, made me feel uneasy. I asked, "Do you have any idea which goddess she is?"

"Yes. Do you know what she is holding in her right hand? A sheaf of wheat." Now that he pointed it out, I could see that the object was indeed a sheaf of wheat, and not a leafy branch. "Wheat symbolizes the Greek Demeter. Historians of ancient Rome wrote that the Etruscans worshiped an underworld goddess corresponding to Demeter. But no one has ever found a statue of her, at least not until now."

"An underworld goddess! I thought she was the earth goddess."

"She was. But wherever she appeared — and such a deity under various names was part of every ancient religion — she had a dual aspect. She was also an infernal goddess. In ancient Arcadia other names for Demeter were 'the black one' and 'the avenger.' She was associated with caves, and springs, and underground waters. Ceremonies in her honor, complete with sacrifice, were held in caves."

He paused, and then added, "Do you see that object in her left hand? Part of it is broken off, but nevertheless I am sure it is a sacrificial knife."

I said, with that sense of chill uneasiness growing stronger, "Althea must have read all that somewhere, and then imagined how the goddess would look."

"*Althea?* She hasn't the slightest interest in archaeology. I know, because I tried to talk to her about it. And she has only a perfunctory interest in Greek or Roman art, or in any art before the late nineteenth century."

I knew that was so. "Then how do you explain this drawing?"

He said after a long moment, "Perhaps someone else made such an imaginary sketch, and she copied it."

I studied his face. "You don't believe that, do you? And you're worried about something. What is it?"

"Why should I be worried?"

I said, exasperated, "You are, and I want to know why. I have a right to know. She's my sister."

He said reluctantly, "It's this. All archaeological discoveries here are the property of the Italian government. Not reporting such a find, let alone smuggling it out of the country and selling it abroad, is a serious criminal offense. That doesn't keep people from trying it, of course. If Althea made such a find — although it's hard to imagine how she could have — or if she became mixed up with people who found it and decided to dispose of it illegally —"

His voice trailed off. I felt sick. Althea mixed up with art thieves? Surely not. But then the Althea I knew would not have let her geraniums die, or debased her talent.

He said, "But I don't think you should worry about it, Samantha. Probably the first explanation I gave you is the real one. Althea knows a lot of people. It could well be that one of them has read of the Etruscan underworld goddess, and asked her to make a sketch of what such a goddess might look like."

I said nothing. After a moment he went on, "It would be simple for anyone with a little knowledge of Roman historical literature and of Etruscan sculpture to have imagined such a statue. In the Archaeological Museum in Florence there are many figures wearing that hair style and the same sort of garment."

He paused. "Don't you believe me? I can prove it to you. Will you let me take you to that museum in Florence? You might feel better afterward."

"Yes, I'd appreciate that."

"Shall we say day after tomorrow, in the afternoon? I'd say tomorrow afternoon, except that I don't want to have to rush you home so you can primp for your date with Arturo Rafaello."

Despite my worry over Althea, a certain wryness in his tone made me want to smile. "All right," I said, "day after tomorrow."

We said good-bye. I took the sketch of that enigmatic figure upstairs. Then Caesar and I set off through the olive grove. It was near sunset now. Reddish light, striking between the breeze-stirred leaves, lay in shifting patches on the coarse grass and ocher-clay earth. We criss-crossed the grove several times. Nowhere did I see what I had feared to see — some sign that the ground had been disturbed.

Finally we emerged from the grove on the far side from the farmhouse. Ahead the ground sloped gently upward, dotted with cypress trees and strewn with scarlet poppies that stood even taller than the wild grass. We climbed to the hill's crest. Ahead, on the other side of a small brook flowing down to join the river I had first seen from the farmhouse window, was a taller hill, with a thick stand of cypress about halfway up it. Was it, too, part of the Rafaellos' land? Probably, since they owned two hundred acres.

I was sure that Althea must have climbed that hill and painted the landscape stretching before her, back in the days before she started turning out Duomos and Ponte Vecchios by the score. The Rafaellos' villa would be visible from there. Perhaps from that vantage point she could even see the walled town from which our maternal ancestors had sprung. I could imagine her standing at her easel up there, biting her full underlip, as I had so often seen her do when concentrating hard, or stepping back to run her left hand through her mane of dark red hair when she was pleased with her work.

Soon it would be dark. We turned and hurried back toward the farmhouse and that reassuring gun in the nightstand drawer beside the bed.

9

My groceries and my twenty kilos of ice both arrived before eleven the next morning. Once I had stowed away the food in the cupboard and icebox, I descended the stairs and began to clean out the old stable so that I could drive my car into it safely. Using the wooden rake, I uncovered enough old nails and broken glass on the straw-strewn dirt floor to make me glad that until now I had left the Simca standing out in the yard.

I drove the car into one side of the stable and then, after crossing to the other side, picked up that pile of old magazines and paperbacks and carried them upstairs. Seated cross-legged on the bedroom floor, I looked through them.

As I have intimated, Althea had never gone in for heavy reading. Consequently I was not surprised at the nature of the books and magazines — copies of the Italian edition of *Mademoiselle* and other popular American and English publications, and English-language paperbacks ranging from Jacqueline Susann through Harold Robbins and Mickey Spillane to something called *All the Loose Ladies*, composed of biographies of famous courtesans, and *The Terror Merchants*, an account of American gangsters with names like No-Nose Scalesi and Three-Finger Thompson.

What did surprise me was that all this reading matter was secondhand. Each book and magazine bore the rubber stamp of a used bookshop in Florence, with the price, a tiny fraction of the original one, written in pencil. What's more, they were badly worn. The binding of *Valley of the Dolls* was so loose that when I picked the book up, several pages fell out. The book about gangsters had a chapter missing — a chapter devoted, according to the table of contents, to one Johnny the Boot. Harold Robbins' *The Dream Merchants* was so old that many of the yellowed pages had broken off at the corners. Someone — I was sure it had not been Althea — had clipped recipes from several of the magazines.

My sister had never been extravagant, but neither had she been miserly. The Althea I knew had not felt it necessary to buy reading matter which was — not just secondhand, apparently — but fourth or fifth hand.

Money. How had it come to play such a

big part in her life? So big that she not only degraded her fine talent, but economized in petty ways. I gathered up the books and magazines and, standing on a chair, placed them atop the tall old wardrobe.

For more than an hour after that Caesar and I wandered over the ground which, south of the house, sloped down to the river. As we moved through poppy-strewn tall grass and past long-neglected peach trees, some hung with a few tiny peaches, I again kept looking for any sign of disturbed earth. I realized, though, that in all probability my haphazard search was senseless. True, it was reasonable to assume that the two guardians of the law stationed in that little hilltop town were far from being topflight detectives. But even so, they had at least some expertise. If they, searching the area around the farmhouse, had found nothing, it was highly doubtful that I would.

For a while I stood on the willow-grown bank of the river. It was at least one hundred feet wide and, to judge by its dark green shade in midstream, quite deep. I watched it for a while as it moved swiftly to join the Arno, and from there to flow to the Ligurian Sea.

Finally I looked at my watch. Past

four-thirty. Time to return to the house and start primping, in my English neighbor's irritated phrase, for my date with Arturo Rafaello. I had brought only one long dress with me, a blue and white cotton print with an off-the-shoulder neckline and a matching shawl. I hoped it would be sufficiently festive.

Before going upstairs, I looked in the mailbox, just as I had that morning. It was empty.

Promptly at seven, a dark red Alfa Romeo turned into the farmyard. Watching from the window, I saw Arturo, in blue blazer and gray flannel trousers, get out of the car and walk toward the foot of the stairs. With Caesar padding beside me, I crossed to the heavy old door and opened it.

At sight of the man climbing the stairs, Caesar gave one deep bark. His tail, though, waved a welcome, perhaps because he remembered that nice behind-the-ears scratch of two afternoons before.

"Hello," Arturo said, and stepped into my kitchen-dining-living room. I smiled at him, again feeling incredulous that any man could be that handsome.

With one hand caressing the shepherd's head, he said, "You look lovely."

"Thank you." I fervently hoped that I did. I hoped that other diners would not ask their companions why that modern Apollo had dated that small girl with the hair-colored hair.

He was looking around the room at the bouquet of poppies I had placed on the table, at the red clay pots, now emptied of their dead geraniums, standing on the windowsills. "Your sister has made this into a really charming room."

"Yes," I said, wondering just how often he had been here.

"Well, shall we go?"

In the sleek red car we drove to Florence through the sunset light, and then up a winding road, bordered by handsome houses set behind terraced gardens, to a huge marble-paved piazza. At one edge of it was an open-air restaurant, with a view of the city's domes and towers and red-tiled roofs spread out below. While the daylight faded and the Venetian glass lanterns strung above the white-clothed tables glowed more brightly, we ate Floren-tine steak — a broiled sirloin sprinkled with lemon juice and olive oil — and drank red wine. Well-dressed women at other tables, I noticed, looked long and admir-ingly at my companion, and enviously and speculatively at me.

As we ate I learned more about Arturo's family. Although that sumptuous villa was more than a hundred years old, it had belonged to the Rafaellos for a far shorter time. Michele Rafaello, a southern Italian who had pyramided a modest inheritance into a fortune by buying up the grapes of vineyards before harvesttime, had bought the villa back in the late nineteen-thirties. As for Arturo's father, who near the end of his life had been made a papal count, he had added to the family fortune by investments in real estate.

"And your mother, the Contessa?"

He explained that she had been a member of an old but untitled banking family, the Vasaris. "As I explained," he said smilingly, "that is how I have done so well in the banking business."

I sensed that he was being too modest. Despite his good looks, there was nothing of the spoiled playboy about him. I was sure that he had inherited his grandfather's and father's shrewd business sense, and gave good value for whatever salary he received.

He said, "Now it is your turn. Please tell me about where you grew up. If I remember correctly, Althea said it had some sort of tree in its name."

"It's called Oak Corners." I spoke of the volunteer — and unpaid — fire department, trying to explain to him how it was that Oak Corners businessmen considered it a great honor to belong, even though it meant tumbling out of their beds whenever the siren atop the town hall shrieked late at night. I spoke of our Fourth of July celebration, complete with the traditional ladies' peanut race — its origins lost in the mists of time — which required the matronly contestants to line up, each holding a teaspoon with a peanut in its bowl. From there, eyes glued to the teaspoons, they raced a hundred feet to the finish line. Any lady whose peanut spilled from the spoon was disqualified. Arturo's face held the fascinated look of one hearing about the customs of some Amazonian tribe.

After dinner we drove down the winding road to one of Florence's few night clubs. It was housed in a huge vaulted room, once the wine cellar of an ancient palace. A violinist and accordionist wandered in and out among the tables, playing Italian love songs. My anxieties faded to the back of my mind. Surrounded by chic Florentines, and listening to that lush music, and watching candlelight waver on the stone arches overhead, I began to feel I had been caught up in a Fellini movie.

Around midnight we started back through the warm darkness. We had just turned onto the broad autostrada when Arturo said, "I gather you have not heard from your sister."

"Not yet." Reminded of Althea, I felt a dimming of the pleasant glow the last few hours had brought me. After a moment I said, "In Florence yesterday I saw some of Althea's recent pictures in a shop."

He glanced at me swiftly. "Oh?"

"You knew the sort of thing she had been painting recently, didn't you?"

He answered, much as Jeffrey had, "Yes, but I didn't want to be the one to tell you. Althea has told me how much you value her talent — overvalue it, she feels."

I did not reply to that. Instead I asked, "Did she ever happen to show you a sketch of a statue?"

"I don't believe so. What sort of statue?"

"Jeffrey Hale says it's Etruscan."

"Dr. Hale, the archaeologist who shares old Domenico Pasquale's house each summer?"

"Yes."

"Then it must be what he says it is. He's a recognized authority on the Etruscans.

But no, Althea never showed me such a drawing."

We drove in silence for a while. Then he said, "I know that American villages don't have patron saints. But don't they each have some famous person to boast of, someone who was born there, or at least slept there?"

"My village doesn't. Not even George Washington's drummer boy slept in Oak Corners, as far as we know. We did have someone who was signed by the Baltimore Colts — that's a football team — but they dropped him before the training season was over."

We talked of Oak Corners the rest of the way to the farmhouse. As we climbed the dark stairs, Caesar barked furiously on the other side of the door. At Arturo's request I fished the key from my crocheted evening bag and handed it to him, aware of the warm touch of his fingers. After a certain amount of fumbling, he unlocked the door and swung it back into the lighted kitchen. Caesar's barks turned into delighted yelps.

"Quiet!" I said. Then to Arturo, "I've had a wonderful evening."

"So have I. Tomorrow morning I must go down to Rome. We have an interest in a vineyard near there. But I shall be back in a few days. Will you have dinner with me then?"

"Of course. I'll look forward to it."

He took my hand and raised it to his lips. "Good night, Samantha. I will see you soon."

I kept the door open to light his way down the stairs. Then I closed it and stood there, listening to the Alfa Romeo start up and drive away. "He'll wine you and dine you and flatter you and try his best to seduce you," Jeffrey had said. "What he won't do is to take you seriously."

And yet Arturo hadn't even tried to kiss my lips. Did that mean that, in spite of the Englishman's prediction, Arturo had decided to treat me "seriously"? Or did it mean that I did not quite measure up to his idea of a beddable girl?

I became aware of my own absurdity. I had feared he would not realize that, where sexual matters were concerned, my standards were quite different from Althea's. But now that his behavior had made it plain that he did realize I was different, I actually felt a little miffed.

I opened the door, let Caesar out for a brief run, and then called him in. Soon after that I went to bed.

I don't know what hour of the night it was when the shepherd's explosive barking awoke me. Heart hammering, I ran through the darkness to that heavy locked door at the head of the stairs, and seized the dog's collar. "Quiet!" I whispered sharply.

Caesar obeyed. I listened. No sound on the stairs. No sound anywhere except for the muffled beat of my own heart. Then, somewhere not far away, a dog let out a fusillade of barks. No doubt wanting to obey me, but unable to resist the other dog's challenge, Caesar let out one sharp yelp.

"And you woke me up for that! Now lie down and go to sleep," I said crossly, and went back to bed.

10

I had been up only a few minutes the next morning when, still wearing my robe, I opened the door to let Caesar out. He raced down the stairs. I started to close the door and then stood motionless, hand on the knob. Early sunlight, penetrating part way up the staircase, showed me something affixed to the right-hand wall. My steps reluctant, I descended the stairs.

It was a sheet of cheap lined paper, evidently torn from a tablet and affixed to the stone wall with a bit of transparent tape. On it was a childish sketch, drawn with crayons, of a figure dangling from a gallows.

With nausea in the pit of my stomach, I realized that the hanged figure was supposed to be me. The shoulder-length hair on the grotesquely lolling head was light brown. The clothes on the dangling body were recognizable as the blue pants and overblouse into which I had changed soon after I arrived at the farmhouse three days before.

Had that repulsive sketch been there

when Arturo and I climbed the dark stairs about eight hours ago? Perhaps. More likely, it had been placed there later. It must have been the sound of stealthy movement on these stairs, rather than another dog's barking, which had aroused Caesar in the night.

I shrank from even touching that thing on the wall. And when I did take it down, I had to fight back the impulse to tear it into bits. I carried it back up the stairs, locked the door, and placed the sketch, facedown, in the drawer of that desk in the bedroom.

I must not be frightened, I told myself. That was what someone wanted. A cowardly someone who twice had invaded this house under cover of darkness, the first time to set that fire — I was sure now that it had been set — and the second time to leave that crude but chilling sketch.

Should I show it to the carabinieri in Isolotta? I doubted that it would do any good. The man who had been here the day before obviously had attached no importance to that fire in the oil drum. He and his colleague would be even less impressed by the sort of drawing a mischievious ten-year-old might have made. I would wait, and ask Jeffrey Hale's advice when he

132

came to take me to Florence.

I started back into the kitchen and then halted, struck by a sudden memory — the apprehension I had felt that first day when I had looked down the stairwell and seen the Englishman's broad shoulders silhouetted against the light. And since then I had had the impression more than once that he was lying to me. In fact, he had admitted that he had lied when he said that he did not know what Florence "gallery" was handling Althea's work.

Nevertheless, I found it hard to imagine an archaeology professor making that childish crayon sketch, and then sneaking onto this property in the dead of night to affix it to the stairwell wall.

Partly to distract myself, I spent the next few hours housecleaning. Fine cobwebs had gathered in corners near the ceiling in the bedroom as well as the kitchen. When I swept down the bedroom walls, I noticed that the cream-colored paint was dingy, and even discolored in spots. I have always enjoyed transforming a room by applying fresh paint. In Florence I could buy some quick-drying paint and set to work here. Althea would not mind. Perhaps, though, I should ask the Rafaellos' permission. After all, I was not even the official tenant here, let alone the owner.

I was dusting the sill of a window facing the road when I saw Jeffrey's Rover turn into the farmyard. Whipping off the scarf I had bound around my head, I went into the bedroom, combed my hair, and then hurried back to answer Jeffrey's knock.

When I opened the door, he said, "Hello, Samantha." Caesar, standing beside me, gave a friendly bark: "Hello, monster." He patted the dog's head and then stepped into the room. "All set?"

"Could you give me ten minutes to clean myself up a bit?"

"Take all the time you want."

"While I'm getting ready, I'd like for you to look at something."

I went into the bedroom, took that crayon drawing from the desk drawer, and walked back into the kitchen to hand it to him. He said after a moment, "What the *hell*."

I told him where I had found it. "I'll change now. It won't take me ten minutes." I went into the bedroom and closed the door. When I emerged, wearing white cotton pants and a yellow tee shirt, I found him seated at the table, fingers drumming its dark surface. He said, "Do you have any idea who could have done this?"

"No. Do you?"

"No. But there's one possible conclusion. This is a nonverbal threat. You might expect a printed 'Take Warning' or 'Get Out' or some such pleasantry at the bottom of the sketch. But there's nothing. That might indicate that whoever made the drawing is illiterate."

I thought of the grim elderly woman who had assembled my groceries in that hilltop village. "Are some of the people in Isolotta illiterate?"

"Quite a few of the older ones are."

"They were hostile the day I was there."

He looked uncomfortable. "They were?"

"Distinctly. I know it must have been because of Althea. Is it just that they think of her as — immoral, or do they have something specific against her?"

His tone was reluctant. "I'm afraid they do, at least some of them. You see, there is a young man there named Carlo Vanezzi, who was engaged to a girl named something-or-other Marchetti. Carlo caught Althea's eye and — well, the upshot was that the girl became angry, and her family even angrier, particularly her grandfather, and the marriage never took place. In a tiny village, with everyone more or less related to everyone else, such things are remembered for a long time."

"I see." Oh, Althea, I thought, you fool.

He picked up the sketch. "Do you want to keep this hideous thing? I don't think there would be any point in showing it to the carabinieri."

I already had come to that conclusion. "Tear it up."

He rose, tore the sheet of paper into bits, and dropped it into the wastebasket beneath the sink. As if to distract me, he said, "What will you do with Caesar while we're gone? He can't go into the museum with us, and I don't imagine you'd want to leave him in the car."

"I'll shut him up in the house."

"Why not leave him outside? Surely he's sufficiently used to the place that he wouldn't wander off."

"I know. But I'm afraid —"

I broke off. He said after a moment, "Afraid that someone in a passing car might toss poisoned meat into the yard?"

"Yes. I suppose you think that's silly."

He glanced at the wastebasket. "No," he said soberly, "I don't think that's silly." Then: "I know. Let's leave him at my place. We'll tie him up on a long rope in the shade, and Domenico will keep him company."

"All right."

A few minutes later, with Caesar in the back seat of the Rover, we drove out of the yard and turned left. After a moment I said, "This Carlo Vanezzi you mentioned. Is his girl's grandfather an old man who wears a yachting cap?"

"Yes. That's Lorenzo Marchetti. How did you know?"

"He said to me —" My throat tightened up. "He said, 'Your sister is a *puttana*.' "

Jeffrey's face swung toward me. Then his right arm went around my shoulders and his hand tightened around my upper arm. "Sticks and stones, Samantha, sticks and stones." He took his arm away. "Try not to be hurt by one word flung at you by an embittered old man."

We turned into the bare yard beside his house. He said, "Wait here. I'll get a rope, and fill a bowl with water."

As he got out of the car, Domenico Pasquale emerged from a doorway and hurried toward us. Jeffrey made the introduction, and then went into the house.

The little old man looked at the politely smiling Caesar. "That'sa one fine dog." His eyes, merry and young-looking in his wizened face, returned to me. "And you one nicea-looking young lady."

"Thank you."

"You knowa the Bronx?"

"I've been there, of course. And my grandparents once lived there." As a young couple they had lived above my grandfather's watch repair shop in what was then a respectable neighborhood in the south Bronx. When my mother was two, they had used their savings to buy a modest house and to open a shop in that little upstate town.

"You ever see-a the Giants?"

"No. I'm afraid I don't know much about baseball." That was a gross understatement. I'm about as well acquainted with baseball as I am with quantum physics.

He said mournfully, "Theya gone now. Theya go to San Francisco."

I said, trying to comfort him, "New York still has the Yankees."

"Yankees!" He spat onto the dirt.

"And there's a newer team, the Mets." Improvising recklessly, I went on, "I think they've won the World Series several times."

The look he gave me, tolerantly amused, made me think that the Mets had not. Then he said, "They winna every game, they stilla not like the Giants."

I changed the subject. "I heard you used to be a jockey. Did you enjoy that?"

He shrugged. "Wassa okay. Base-a-ball much better. But I was too-a short. Too-a short even to catch."

Jeffrey came out of the house just then, a coil of rope over one arm and a water-filled mixing bowl in the other hand. With the voluble Domenico directing the process, we tied Caesar up to the trunk of a mulberry tree. "Be a good dog," I said. "I'll be back in a few hours." Looking reproachful but resigned, Caesar stretched out in the dirt and sunk his head on his paws. Jeffrey and I said good-bye to Domenico, drove out to the road, and turned left toward the autostrada.

Jeffrey asked, "How was your date with young Rafaello?"

"Very pleasant." Unable to resist, I added, "At the end of the evening he unlocked my door for me, kissed my hand, and said good night."

After a moment Jeffrey said, "The bastard's even smoother than I thought."

Plainly he was displeased that Arturo had not made a pass. Did he fear that Arturo might, after all, regard me "seriously"? Looking at the grim profile of the man beside me, I thought, why, I believe's he's jealous. Somehow the idea seemed very pleasant.

"Are you going to see him again?"

"Yes, when he returns from a business trip."

"I think there's something you ought to know about him. He owns some vineyards north of Rome."

"I know that. He told me."

"But I'll bet he didn't tell you that he was mixed up in that wine scandal a few years back. Maybe you heard about it. The government discovered that certain vineyards, among them Rafaello's, were adding the cheapest sort of wine to good-grade wine and selling the mixture as high-priced vintage."

"Was Arturo indicted?"

"Of course not. The Rafaellos are very influential people. His manager took what you Yanks call the rap, which in this case wasn't very much. A few months' imprisonment and a stiff fine. But everyone is sure that young Rafaello knew what was going on."

Maybe he did, I thought, and maybe he didn't.

When I remained silent, Jeffrey said, "Well, aren't you going to repeat it?"

"Repeat what?"

"That remark about male cattiness."

"No, I'm going to heap coals of fire on

your head by telling you that Arturo was very complimentary about you."

"What did he say?"

"That you are a leading authority on the Etruscans."

"Hell, that's no compliment. That's merely the truth."

We left the Rover in the same parking lot I had patronized two days earlier. After crossing the Ponte Vecchio, we continued on through the most ancient part of Florence, past the Piazza della Signoria with its horde of picture-snapping tourists, past the great cathedral and Giotto's Tower, and then past the frowning old Medici palace where Arturo had obtained the gun permit for me. A few minutes later we left a noisy, traffic-clogged street for the churchlike quiet of the Archaeological Museum.

Soon I saw why he had been able to identify instantly that figure in Althea's sketch as Etruscan. Again and again, on stone bas-reliefs and atop sarcophagi, I saw female figures with that same elaborately dressed hair and pleated, flowing garments.

"According to some of the Roman writers," Jeffrey said, "the ancient Etruscans were a licentious lot, whose daily life was like a scenario for an x-rated movie."

As he spoke, I was looking at carved figures, representing a noble and his wife, atop the stone sarcophagus in which their bodies had been laid twenty-five hundred years ago. The man's arm encircled the woman's shoulders. Except for their coiffures and their garments, they might have been some pleasant couple in the New York suburbs posing for a camera held by one of their children.

I said, "I don't believe it. Those two look very respectable."

"Perhaps they were. Perhaps the Romans just cooked up spicy slander about a beaten foe, much as Shakespeare and other Tudor writers painted Richard the Third as black as they could. But we can never know for sure. How can you know much about a person who left no literature? I suppose the Etruscans will always remain a mystery."

A mystery. Like that sketch my sister had made. If the figure in that sketch really existed, it belonged in this museum. Instead, it might be that in her money-hunger she had turned to men who looted this ancient land of its heritage —

He was looking down at me. "I think," he said, "that I have educated you enough for one day. Now I'll take you someplace and feed you."

He did. In a trattoria where the crowd was noisy, the service cheerfully haphazard, and the food excellent, we had an omelette and green salad. After that we went to what in America would be called a hardware store. There I bought a container of quick-drying interior paint and a brush. When we emerged from the store, with Jeffrey carrying my purchases in a cardboard box, I looked to our right and saw a wide cobble-stoned street with several rows of roofed stalls stretching down it. "What's that?"

"The market. Not the Straw Market. That's mainly for tourists. Everybody goes to this one. Want to see it?"

We walked down the rows of stalls. Fruits and vegetables. Pots and pans and cheese graters. Souvenirs of every sort, from mirrors with plaster-of-paris frames to scarves with Giotto's Tower printed on them. Blue jeans and khaki work pants and heavy shoes. Then on one of the barrows I saw a stack of cellophane-wrapped pantyhose. To judge by the tiny price, they were what Americans call seconds. Next to them, propped up against a pile of folded blue jeans, stood one of Althea's paintings of the Duomo. A hand-lettered sign at its foot said, "Specially priced. Genuine original oil painting."

Perhaps that crude sketch of a hanged figure had shaken me even more than I had realized. Or perhaps, much as I had hated to see her work in that souvenir shop, it seemed to me even more devastating to find one of her pictures displayed beside bargain-priced pantyhose. Whatever the reason, I heard myself draw a shuddering breath and felt tears spring to my eyes.

"Come on." Hand holding my elbow, he guided me through two lines of stalls and up the steps of a church. In its shadowy and deserted portico he said, "Okay, let go."

For perhaps two minutes I wept against his shoulder, while he held me and patted me and made soothing noises. Then he mopped the tears from my face with his handkerchief. "Better?"

"Much better."

He tilted my chin and kissed me. "A bit salty," he said, smiling, "but very nice."

I managed to return his smile.

"Do you want to go home now, or would you rather stay here a little longer?"

"Home, please. I intended to order groceries, but now —"

"Make out a list on the way home. I can

phone the market from my house."

We walked back to the parking lot, drove out of Florence, and joined the stream of traffic on the autostrada. Using a small pad of paper and a pencil from the Rover's glove compartment, I made out my grocery list.

I said, "I need ice, too. It's melting awfully fast. I suppose I should drive in to Isolotta tomorrow."

He threw me a swift glance. "No need for that. I'll order it for you over the telephone."

"Thank you."

When I had placed the paper pad, its top sheet bearing my list, in the glove compartment, he said, "A University of Bologna professor who is visiting Florence is driving out to see me tonight. But I could call him and put him off. Then you and I could have dinner someplace."

"Don't put him off. We can have dinner some other night."

He said after a moment, "Then you're determined to stay on here."

"Yes, until I'm in touch with Althea." I paused. "You still think I should leave?"

"Yes. Not that I think you're in any real danger. I may be wrong, but it seems to me that whoever made that drawing and set that fire — if it was set — is bent on nothing more than harassment. After all, he must have known that your dog would smell the smoke and awaken you in time. Just the same, staying here must be a great strain for you, and so I think you should leave."

I looked at him. Although I felt a growing liking for him, I could not ignore the disturbing conviction that he knew more about my sister than he had admitted. I burst out, "Are you sure it isn't for your own sake that you want me to go? Maybe you feel I ask too many questions."

Those brilliant blue eyes threw me a startled glance. Then he said quietly, facing straight ahead, "Don't be a fool, Samantha. Surely you must realize that under other circumstances the last thing I would want would be for you to leave. But even if you do go back to the States, I'll see you again, and soon. I've been invited to give some guest lectures near New York in August — at a summer session at Yale, to be exact. I've decided to accept the invitation."

"I'm glad." Somewhat to my surprise, I found I was very pleased indeed. "But I won't go home until I've found out where my sister is, and how she is."

He didn't answer.

We turned off the autostrada onto a wide

feeder road, then onto a narrower one, then onto the one, still more narrow, that led past Althea's farmhouse to Domenico's.

Caesar greeted us warmly. So did Domenico. As soon as we stepped from the car, he began to show me yellowed newspaper clippings and a snapshot. The clippings concerned his career as a jockey. One included a photograph of him standing small and bandy-legged beside a sleek thoroughbred in the winner's circle at Belmont. The snapshot had been taken by an usher at the Polo Grounds. It showed a beaming young Domenico standing beside the immortal John McGraw.

We managed to get away from him finally and, with Caesar in the Rover's rear seat, drove back to Althea's place. We had just gotten out of the car when Jeffrey said, "There comes the mail truck."

I watched it approach, my heart beating hard with the illogical hope that Althea had somehow learned I was here, and that the mail carrier would stop and place a letter from her in the box. "See you soon, Sammy darling. In the meantime, hold the fort."

The truck drove past.

"Don't look like that," Jeffrey said. "You'll find her."

11

Before noon the next day I drove to the Rafaello villa, intending to ask the Contessa for permission to paint the bedroom walls. The same aged manservant opened the door and greeted me by name.

"Is the Contessa in?"

The Contessa and her daughter, he told me, had gone to Florence. Only the Contessa's father-in-law was at home.

"Then may I see Signor Rafaello?" Surely he would be able to decide such a trivial matter.

"I am sorry, but the signore seldom sees anyone."

"I would disturb him only for a minute or two. You see, I'd like to have permission to paint one of the rooms at the farmhouse."

The servant hesitated and then said, "Perhaps in that case you had better see him. He is down at the swimming pool."

I followed him across the statue-ornamented entrance hall, through the richly furnished salon, and out onto the broad marble terrace. From there I could see, at the foot of a landscaped slope, the bright green rectangle of the pool. Another uniformed servant, a much younger man, stood beside the iron ladder at the pool's edge, a white terry-cloth robe over his arm. In the pool, bald head well out of the water, Michele Rafaello swam with awkward overhand strokes.

The butler said, "Just go down the steps, Signorina Develin."

I thanked him, and he bowed and turned away. I went down the terrace's broad marble steps and then began to descend the narrower ones that led to the pool. Apparently the old man had seen now that he had a visitor, because he was swimming toward the ladder. He reached it just as I stepped onto the marble-paved area around the pool. The servant extended a hand and helped him to the pool's edge. Then the old man's foot slipped on the wet surface. If the servant had not caught him, he would have fallen.

Signor Rafaello, his massive head contrasting with his thin and leathery body, said something low and angry. Hastily the servant draped the robe around the deeply tanned old shoulders and then moved rapidly up the stairs to the house.

Michele Rafaello took a couple of limping steps toward me. I cried, "Oh, I'm sorry! You've hurt your foot."

He stopped moving. His dark eyes, deep-set under bushy gray brows, glared at me. He said in Italian, "What do you want?"

Perhaps he was in pain from the near fall. I said, as pleasantly as I could, "I'll stay only a minute. I'm Samantha Develin, Althea Develin's sister, and right now I'm staying at the farmhouse your family owns. I was wondering if —"

"I guessed who you are. What do you want?"

I said stiffly, "The walls in the bedroom are dingy. I was wondering if I might paint them — at my own expense, of course."

"Never mind the walls. Just get out. Go back to America."

Anger speeded my pulse beats. "I paid your daughter-in-law a month's advance rent. I have a perfect right to stay in that house."

"Don't talk about rights, you foolish girl. Just leave. No one wants you here."

I know it was wrong of me. He was very old, and probably in pain from that slip at the pool's edge. But my overstrained nerves must have snapped, because I said, "Your grandson does not seem adverse to my presence. We had a very pleasant dinner together the other night."

An angry flushed dyed his face and then drained away, leaving his face muddy-looking beneath its deep tan. "I know about that dinner. You stay away from my grandson."

So that was it. This old man, father of a papal count, grandfather of a girl who was about to become a princess, wanted his handsome grandson to have nothing to do with me, not even to the extent of taking me to dinner. Perhaps it was not just because I was Althea's sister. Perhaps to him a little American nobody would have been beyond the pale in any event. In short, he was a snob.

The odd part was that I knew from his own grandson that he was of humble origin. Or perhaps it was not odd. Self-made men are often the most ambitious socially for their children and grandchildren.

I said, "I think I'll leave it up to Arturo as to whether we see each other again or not."

He glared at me in silence and then limped back to the ladder, grasped one curved side of it to steady himself, and turned to face me. Suddenly I was ashamed of myself. He was trembling visibly now, and rubbing the instep of his injured foot against the spindly calf of his other leg.

"There's nothing to worry about, Signor Rafaello. I have no designs on your grandson."

"If you know what's good for you, you'll just go back where you belong."

A threat, but a pathetically feeble one. A small child, probably, could have pushed him over.

I looked to my left. From near the other end of the pool a graveled path led up the slope and around the corner of the villa. I would leave that way, rather than walk back through the house.

"I'm sorry you feel that way, Signor Rafaello. Please ask the Contessa to send me a message if she has any objection to my painting the walls. Otherwise I will go ahead."

He made no answer. I turned and followed the path around the villa to where Caesar waited in the Simca.

12

No message from the Contessa arrived that day nor the morning of the next, and so early in the afternoon I pushed and hauled until I had all the bedroom furniture in the center of the room and then set to work with my paintbrush. The paint dried rapidly in the arid heat. By five o'clock, when Jeffrey dropped by to ask me to dinner that night, I was already trying to move the furniture back into place. He restored the room to rights, and then pedaled off to his house to change.

We had dinner that night at a Florence restaurant, its walls frescoed with scenes from the *Decameron*, on one of those narrow, winding streets with practically no sidewalk. As if by tacit consent, we made no mention of Althea. Instead we talked of the lectures he intended to give at Yale, and of my own classes at the private school in Manhattan. Around eleven, under a pale half moon, we drove back to the farmhouse. When we opened the door into the big main room, where I had left the lamp burning, we both patted Caesar. Then

Jeffrey grinned down at me and said, "Sorry I can't kiss your hand. On me it would look silly."

He kissed my lips. "Good night, Samantha."

For the next few days I did housework, read Althea's old magazines and paperbacks, and wandered with Caesar over the land adjoining the house. Once I cooked lunch for Jeffrey and myself. He moved the wrought-iron table and chairs into the shade of the old orange tree so that we could have our meal on the terrace. Another afternoon we drove into Florence, and joined the crowd of tourists moving through the Uffizi's art-crammed rooms and long corridors.

Every afternoon, heart quickening with hope, I looked in the mailbox or watched the approaching mail truck. There was never any word from Althea, or about her. Arturo sent a postcard from Rome, though, saying that business would keep him there a little longer than he had expected, but that he would be home for his sister's wedding on the tenth, and he hoped I would have dinner with him on the following night.

It was two days after I received that postcard that I found the Etruscan goddess. Or rather, Caesar found her.

At least twice before I had climbed that hill, the second and taller of the two hills directly east of the farmhouse. Each time I had skirted around the copse of cypress trees about halfway up the slope, a copse so thick that some of the cypress had not survived. Their tops, bare and brown, showed here and there among the solid dark green mass of the grove. I had noticed, too, the few roughly hewn stones — probably limestone — scattered down the slope below the copse. I had attached no importance to them. After all, they might have been the remains of some wall marking off an ancient field or pasture land.

On that particular late afternoon, though, Caesar chose to give chase to some small animal. I never knew what it was. Not a rabbit, because it scurried away close to the ground, its swift flight marked by a moving furrow through the tall grass and scarlet poppies. Perhaps it was some sort of weasel. Because I see no reason why well-fed dogs should harry other creatures, I tried to call him back, but already he had disappeared into that mass of thickly grown trees.

I waited there in the hot sunlight. For a while I heard the sound of breaking branches. Then silence. I called again. Still only silence. I hesitated, reluctant to try to make my way through those interlaced branches and the undergrowth beneath.

Then I had a sudden vision of Caesar, with his collar caught on a stout branch, strangling himself in his effort to get free. I ran forward, calling his name, and plunged into the copse, one arm crooked in front of my face to ward off lashing branches.

There was even more undergrowth than I had anticipated. It caught at my jean-clad legs and scratched my bare ankles. There were more of those rough-hewn white stones, too, lying at the bases of tree trunks that had arrested their downward plunge. Pausing now and then to call Caesar, moving now this way and now that, I made my way up through the copse.

Abruptly I emerged onto a slanting apron of grassy earth. Beyond and above it was an irregular opening in the hillside. Along the bottom of the opening a few of those stones were still in place, forming a low, uneven wall. Caesar, pursuing his quarry, must have leapt those stones. I climbed a few more feet and looked inside the opening.

A cave. Even before my eyes adjusted to the dim light, I could see, standing against the grayish rear wall, and close to a blackness I knew must mark a passage to a deeper part of the cave, something about five feet tall, something that faintly gleamed.

Almost at once I guessed that I had found her. The Etruscan Demeter in her infernal aspect, goddess of caves, and springs, and underground waters. I neither saw nor heard a trickling spring, but I caught the cool smell of water, perhaps from somewhere along that passage leading deeper into the hill.

I stared at her, feeling the hair on the back of my neck prickle, feeling an atavistic stir of the awe and fear that some ancestress of mine, dead more than two thousand years, must have felt as she approached the goddess. Then I placed one knee on the remains of the wall and, dislodging another of the rough stones in the process, scrambled over the low barrier. I had little fear that bats might fly out at me from that dark passageway. This cave had been reopened to the light of day much too recently, I felt sure, for bats to have taken up residence.

I stood before her. Holding life-sustaining wheat in one hand and the fragment of the death-dealing knife in the other, she smiled at me her mysterious and chilling smile. Greenish mold splotched her face and her flowing garments, but these marks of her long isolation seemed only to add to her impressiveness. From the ragged opening, about six feet high and two feet wide, near her in the cave's rear wall, a current of damp air struck me.

Who had sealed her up? Early Christians of this region? Probably. Still half pagan, they had been afraid to destroy her, or even remove her from her cave, and so they had walled her up, hoping to seal off her power from the world of living men.

It was a natural force, I was sure, which had ended her centuries-long entombment. According to Jeffrey, the recent earthquake which had all but destroyed towns in northern Italy had sent strong tremors into Tuscany. The ancient and unmortared wall, collapsing, had broken through the crust of earth covering it. Stones had spilled down through the closely packed cypress, a few coming to rest below the copse.

Many times during her years at the farmhouse, Althea must have climbed this hill to its crest. Then on a day some months back she must have seen something that had not been there before —

primitively hewn stones scattered below the grove. I imagined her struggling through the trees and seeing, as I had, still more stones. Finally she must have stood where I now stand.

I pictured her rushing back to the farm and returning to the cave with sketch pad and charcoal. And after that? Perhaps she had shown the sketch to someone, someone she had reason to think would help her profit from her find. Had she told him its location? Almost certainly not. Otherwise the statue would not be here.

I heard Caesar's bark reverberating hollowly from somewhere deeper in the hillside. Staring into that green-splotched bronze face, I had forgotten all about him. I called, and after a moment he emerged from the black mouth of the passageway, tail drooping, face guilty. He leaped over the remains of the wall. I too scrambled across it, and fought my way through the copse and into the warm sunlight of late afternoon.

As I moved toward the farmhouse, with the shepherd running ahead, I asked myself what I should do. Tell the Archaeological Museum in Florence? Tell Jeffrey? But what if that led to the discovery that Althea had been involved in some sort of scheme to dispose of the statue illegally? I must tell no one, not until I found her, not until I learned whether or not that smiling bronze figure had anything to do with my sister's puzzling and tormenting absence.

When I reached the farmyard, I went automatically and with little hope to the mailbox.

But this time there was a letter inside. Not from Althea, I saw with a rush of disappointment, but to her, the address written in a large but feminine hand. It had been mailed from Milan, with the return address printed on the flap of the heavy blue envelope. Unhesitatingly, I opened the letter.

Someone had written in Italian:

Dear Althea,

I have been hoping to hear from you or, better yet, see you. Are you off on a trip somewhere?

You are greatly missed here. Your friends frequently ask for you. And there are others who want to meet you. As soon as you receive this, please write to me, or telephone.

Sincerely,
Francesca Bellini

Filled with new hope, I read the letter twice. There was something puzzling and even disturbing about it, but no matter. At least I had an address now, and the name of someone who apparently knew Althea well, and was in touch with others who knew her.

Should I telephone? No, I decided. I knew nothing of this woman, nor her relation to Althea. If I phoned her, she might very well put me off. Best to go there as soon as I could. If I left the next morning, I could be in Milan by noon or a little later.

But what if I had to wait to see her, and as a consequence was detained in Milan overnight? Few hotels in any city would take in a dog of Caesar's size, and I didn't know whether or not I would find a motel in Milan. Best to leave Caesar in Jeffrey's care.

But I would not tell Jeffrey about the letter. He had lied to me — I was convinced of it — when he assured me he did not know the reason for Althea's frequent trips to Milan. He might even know something about this Francesca Bellini, something that would make him try to prevent my seeing her. And if he failed in that, he might phone her a warning of my arrival.

No, best to keep silent, not only about the bronze figure but this letter. Right now I was groping my way through a fog of unanswered questions. Best to wait until the fog lifted a little before I put full trust in anyone. Otherwise I might discover, too late, that in trying to find my sister I had betrayed her.

I thrust the letter into the pocket of my jeans. Then I went upstairs, collected Caesar's bag of dry dog food and his dinner bowl and blanket and leash, and came down again. With Caesar beside me I drove through the sunset light to Domenico's house, trying not to think of that bronze face, or that enigmatic letter, or of anything except what I would say to Jeffrey.

No one was in the hard-packed yard. I went through a doorless opening and looked up ancient stairs to a landing with a door on either side. Since I had never visited Jeffrey's quarters, I did not know whether he lived in the front or the rear of the house. But the odor of warm olive oil, and the sound of a cracked recording of Pagliacci's Sob Song, seemed to come from the door leading to the rear. That door, surely, belonged to the ex-jockey and loyal Giant fan. I climbed the stairs and knocked on the door opposite.

The sound of a typewriter ceased. After a moment the door opened. Jeffrey said, "Samantha! Come in."

I stepped past him into a room furnished with a studio couch covered in dark red monk's cloth and a few mismatched chairs. On a desk of scarred blond wood, a green-shaded student lamp cast a pool of light on a portable typewriter and the telephone beside it.

"I'm sorry to interrupt you."

"I'm glad you did. When I'm writing, any interruption is welcome."

"Writing?"

"A piece for *The Archaeological Review*. One of those publish-or-perish articles that are the bane of a professor's life." His tone altered. "Is something wrong?"

"No. It's just that I wondered if you would take care of Caesar tomorrow, and perhaps the next day."

"Of course. But why?"

"I want to drive up to Milan."

His eyes narrowed. "What for?"

"To see the police there. After all, that's where Althea's car was found, near the Milan railroad station. I also thought I might ask the ticket sellers and porters at the station if they remembered anyone like her."

"Samantha, that's foolish. If the Milan

police had any more news, they would have gotten in touch with the carabinieri in Isolotta. And what makes you think that you might find someone at the station who remembers her? The police couldn't, and they are experts at jogging memories."

"I can try."

He studied me. "Are you sure you don't have some other reason for going? Have you heard from Althea, or from someone who knows her?"

"No."

"Maybe you're telling the truth, but if you're not, let me give you some advice. Only an inexpert liar looks directly and belligerently into the other person's eyes, as you are doing now."

I said stubbornly, "I am not lying."

He gave it up then. "All right, I'll keep him. But if you're not back by tomorrow night, will you telephone me? I'll write down the number."

"Yes."

"Promise?"

"Yes."

"Then I might as well drive back to your place right now and collect Caesar."

"You don't have to. He's downstairs. I brought his food and his bowl and his blanket, too."

He smiled. "Sure of yourself, weren't you?"

No, I thought, feeling forlorn and obscurely frightened, I was not sure of myself, or him, or anyone else. All I knew was that I must find Althea.

13

In Milan early the next afternoon I drove slowly along a wide residential street. The houses lining it were large and set well back behind walled gardens, but the ones along this stretch appeared less well cared for than those I previously had passed. Glazed tiles were missing from garden walls. Through gateways I caught glimpses of lawns that needed mowing and trees with dead branches. Twice I saw for-sale signs. The houses still were fine ones. With their mansard roofs and gray stone façades, they reminded me of photographs I had seen of rich residential areas in Paris.

Nerves tightening, I saw the number I sought affixed to a gatepost. I parked at the curb and got out. This place was far better kept than its neighbors'. As I moved up a cement walk, I saw that the beds of snapdragons and foxgloves bordering it were weedless. The freshly mown lawn was green and velvety, and on all three floors dormered windows sparkled in the light.

I mounted marble steps and pushed a button beside a door of frosted glass. After a moment a swarthly, middle-aged maid in a black alpaca dress and white apron and cap opened the door. At sight of me her welcoming smile gave way to a surprised look.

"Is Signora Bellini in?"

She hesitated, and then asked, "What name shall I say?"

"Develin, Samantha Develin. I'm Althea Develin's sister."

She stared at me silently for a moment. "Please wait," she said.

Standing there on the doormat, I watched her walk a few feet down a marble-floored hall and then turn to her left through an archway. Opposite the archway was the foot of a staircase leading upward toward a shadowy landing.

There was a murmur of voices. Finally the maid returned. "This way, please." She led me to the archway and then walked on down the hall.

Evidently its window shades were half drawn, because the big room beyond the archway looked cool and shadowy. In a far corner a woman, back turned to me, was bent over an old man slumped in an armchair. "Wake up, Father," I heard her say. With obvious effort the old man got up, opened a door a few feet behind his chair, and left the room. It was only then that the woman turned and walked toward me.

She was about fifty, I saw, a handsome woman with a well-corseted figure in a gray shirtwaist frock of some satiny material. If her piled hair was dyed, then her hairdresser must have been an expert, because its dark brown shade looked entirely natural.

"I am Francesca Bellini."

I took the hand she extended. It was cool and dry. "Samantha Develin."

"Won't you sit down?"

As I moved toward a sofa of dark green velvet, I gained a more distinct impression of the room. Overstuffed furniture that undoubtedly was expensive, but too rich and heavy for my taste. A grand piano ornamented in *belle époque* fashion with a fringed Spanish shawl and an enormous bouquet of white roses in a silver bowl. Over the marble-manteled fireplace was a large and not very good copy of Titian's reclining Venus, admiring her face in the mirror a fat cupid held for her. There was something strange about Signora Bellini's living room, just as there had been about her letter.

She sat down in an upholstered chair facing me. "So you are Althea's sister. You do not look at all like her." The tone was pleasant enough, but her dark eyes were watchful.

"I know."

"How is Althea?"

"I don't know." My throat tightened. "I don't even know where she is. I thought you might be able to help me."

She did not answer that directly. Instead, after a moment she asked, "How is it you have come here?"

"It was the letter you sent to her." I explained about the Contessa's transatlantic phone call, and my long and fruitless wait at the farmhouse. "When your letter came addressed to Althea, I opened it. I thought it might help me to find her."

"I see." There was a long silence, broken only by the ticking of a green marble clock on the mantelpiece. Then she said, "I have not seen your sister for about three months. I have no idea where she is."

Disappointment held me silent for several seconds. Then I said, "Could you give me the names of some of her friends? Perhaps one of them has heard from her within the last few days."

"Friends?"

"The ones you mentioned in your letter. You said that they had been asking about her."

"I'm sure they have no idea where she is, either." There was dismissal in her tone. "My best advice would be for you to return to her house and wait for her."

I said, "Are you sure you have no idea where I might —"

"No."

Again silence settled down. Then on the floor above a door opened and closed. A couple descending the stairs came into my line of vision. The girl, a blonde, was in a loose, brightly patterned kaftan. The man, middle-aged and turning to fat, wore a dark business suit. Three-quarters of the way down the stairs they stopped. The man said something to the girl in a low voice. She giggled and moved lightly back up the stairs.

My hostess said quickly, getting to her feet, "You must excuse me now. Perhaps it would be best if you went out that other door —"

But already the man in the dark suit stood in the archway. He said jovially, "Well! Who is this?"

"No one who could possibly concern you," Signora Bellini said. Her tone was pleasant but firm. "Good day, signore."

He looked at me again. He opened his mouth as if to say something and then shrugged and walked away. I heard the front door open and close.

I felt as if a band were tightening around my chest. It was an effort for me to ask, "What sort of place —"

"I think you have guessed." Her tone was cold and sharp, but there was a hint of sympathy in her dark eyes. "Perhaps this will teach you, my girl, not to open other people's mail."

I ignored that. "Did Althea ever — live here?"

"No. My clients include some of the richest and most prominent men in Milan, as well as men from other cities who come to Milan for business reasons. Consequently mine must be a very quiet and discreet establishment. I never have more than three girls living here. But others, like Althea, come in for a few afternoons in a row, or a few evenings."

Strange that my eyes as well as my lips were dry when I was crying so hard inside. "But why —"

"For money." She shrugged. "What other reason would she have?"

"But how can she possibly need money so badly that —"

"Because of a man, of course." Her tone was sardonic. "Your sister is in love. In fact, she told me that Federico Scazzi is the first man she ever really loved."

"Who is he?"

"Once he was a young architect — a brilliant one, I heard. Then about seven years ago he became an addict. He has been on and off heroin ever since. When Althea met him — oh, more than four years ago — he was off drugs. But that didn't last long."

Althea, I thought. My sister, with her too-great tenderness for losers and weaklings.

"In all, she has paid for three cures for him, very expensive ones. Between cures she has kept him supplied with dope, which also is very expensive. She heard of me, somehow, and came to me, quite desperate, about eighteen months ago. I agreed to introduce her to a few of my clients."

I sat silent, hands gripped in my lap.

"Your sister is older than my other girls," she went on, "but nevertheless she is very popular with my customers. I suppose there's a certain charm and distinction about her that strikes them as a novelty."

Distinction. "Distinguished" was one of the adjectives an art critic used in his review of a small show of hers in a Madison Avenue gallery. "Althea Develin, a distinguished young painter greatly influenced by Impressionism —" Oh, God, I thought.

Aloud I said, "Might this Federico Scazzi know where she is?"

"Not unless he's learned something within the last few days. When I telephoned him last week, he said that he had neither seen nor heard from her for more than two months."

"Do you have his address?"

She said after a moment, "Are you sure you want to see him?"

"Yes."

"My advice still is to go back to Althea's place. Better yet, go back to New York and your teacher friends. That's where you belong."

So Althea had told her I taught school.

"But since you've seen me," she went on, "I suppose you might as well see Scazzi too. And it might be that he knows something."

She got up and crossed the room to a spindly-legged desk of dark wood ornamented with brass scrollwork. She wrote something on a pad, ripped off the top page, and then opened the desk drawer. When she walked back to me, she was carrying not only the slip of paper but a folded map. "Here's his address. You'll need a street map to find it."

I don't remember saying good-bye to her or even leaving the house. I do remember leaning against the tiled garden wall and fighting down the need to be sick right there on the sidewalk. Finally I got into the Simca, drove a hundred yards or so from that house, and again pulled into the curb. I crossed my arms over the steering wheel and sank my head upon them.

Long before this, I realized now, I had been aware of Althea's reckless streak. When she came home to Oak Corners from Manhattan on weekends and spoke casually of men she had met in singles bars, I had felt a twinge of anxiety. What if she learned, too late, that the stranger she had met in such a place was evil and dangerous? But dazzled as I was by her, I'd had to go on thinking that anything Althea did must be all right.

Besides, frequenting singles bars was a vast distance from becoming one of Signora Bellini's girls. And yet in the seven years since I had last seen her, Althea had traveled that distance.

Had something irreversibly destructive happened to Althea during her childhood, those first twelve years of her life before my own birth? Had one or both of those parents I could not remember so undermined her self-esteem that, later on, her only real interest was in men unworthy of her? Certainly that had been her pattern. And now this Federico Scazzi, a weakling for whose sake she had demeaned her talent and, finally, her body.

But I had never received any indication from her or from our grandparents that her childhood had been anything except normal and happy. Certainly she always had spoken of our parents with deep affection. Perhaps because she wanted me to share her memories of them, she often told me of the times she and our mother had gone down to our father's law office above the Merchants and Farmers Bank, so that he could take them to lunch at the Oak Corners Hotel. She spoke too of birthday parties on the lawn, with our father doing magic tricks for her small guests, and of how, from the age of seven on, she often had ridden with our parents in the sports car in which they ultimately crashed to their deaths.

No, probably there was nothing in her childhood to explain why she was so self-destructive — why, for the sake of a heroin addict, she had turned out all those mechanical, joyless paintings, and spent all those hours in Francesca Bellini's house. Perhaps the human soul had some mysteries that not even psychologists could explain.

One thing I was sure of. Jeffrey Hale had heard rumors about Althea and the Bellini house. That must have been why he had urged me to go back to New York. He had wanted to keep me from knowing what I had learned today.

I raised my head finally, and spread out the map, and started searching for Federico Scazzi's street.

14

Less than half an hour later I parked the Simca in front of an apartment house, one of a row of tan brick buildings, where Federico Scazzi lived. There was nothing unusual about it. In fact, I imagine that such dull, utilitarian-looking structures have risen in about every city in the world in the past few decades. The small lobby had a black marble floor, though, and black marble stairs leading upward. But then, marble is plentiful and cheap enough in Italy to be used in even low-cost construction.

A row of mailboxes stretched along one wall. In the slot above box 3-B was a card with Scazzi's name on it, hand-printed in ink. I climbed the stairs, meeting no one, but hearing the mingled sounds of radios and TV sets playing behind the thin doors. When I found the door marked 3-B, I pushed the bell beside it.

Quick footsteps. The door opened wide. A tall man of about thirty-five stood there. At sight of me, an avid eagerness vanished from his face, leaving it disappointed, almost stricken. Who was it, I wondered, that he had expected to see?

"Signor Scazzi?"

"Yes."

"I'm Samantha Develin."

"Althea's sister?" From his tone, only slightly interested and curious, I gathered that it was not Althea he had hoped to find standing there.

"That's right."

"Come in."

The small square living room, its shades drawn, was even dimmer than Francesca Bellini's salon had been. But enough yellowish light came through the blinds to show me that the room, although neat, was almost as characterless as the display window of a third-rate furniture store. No books or magazines. No pictures on the wall. Just the cheap blond furniture which, in all probability, was supplied to tenants by the management.

He said, "Sit down." As I sat down in a chair with a blue monk's cloth covered cushion and open wooden arms, he added, "I hope you don't mind the shades. I've got a headache." To judge by his pallor and the jerkiness of his speech, more than a headache ailed him.

He sat down facing me on the open-armed settee. He was a good-looking man, or at least had been. An olive-skinned, even-featured face. Dark eyes deeply circled underneath. Dark brown hair waving back from a broad forehead. The effect was that of a ravaged Lord Byron.

He said, "How is Althea? And how is it she sent you instead of coming here herself?"

So apparently he had no recent information about her. Disappointment held me silent for a moment. Then I said, "I don't know how she is. I don't even know where she is. I've been trying to find out ever since I came to Italy from New York more than ten days ago."

He said, puzzled, "If she didn't send you, then how is it you knew about me? Did she mention me in her letters?"

"No." I waited until I could speak matter-of-factly. "A woman named Bellini wrote to Althea at the farmhouse. I opened the letter, and came up here to see her. She told me about you."

Something resembling embarrassment came into his face. "I guess she told you quite a lot about me."

"A few things. But I'm interested only in finding my sister. Do you have any idea where she is?"

"No. The last time she was here was in early April. She said she was going away to close some sort of deal and then come back here. I've been waiting for her ever since."

"Where was she going?"

"She didn't tell me." His eyes, I saw now, were watering slightly. Sinus trouble? Almost instantly I realized it was not. These were symptoms I had heard of, the symptoms of an addict with nerves screaming for more heroin.

"Please tell me all you know about my sister."

"Well, she and I were — are — engaged. We've been planning to go to the States after we marry. As her husband, I'd automatically become a citizen. Even so, Immigration would check me over — and, well, I have this problem. I've had it almost ten years now —"

Afraid that he was about to wander off down a bypath, I said, "I know about that. Althea has been hoping that if she made enough money, your problem could be cured permanently."

He nodded. "We figured that if I could stay in the sanitarium for six months the next time, or even a year — But that costs a lot of money, even more than —"

180

He broke off, but I knew what he meant. Private sanitariums cost even more than heroin.

He went on, "When I last saw her, she was hoping to make a deal that would bring her a lot of money all at once."

"Was it a deal about this statue she'd found?"

He looked startled. "No, that was earlier. That didn't work out. The person she hoped would help her wouldn't go for the idea. I don't know who it was. Althea doesn't confide in me completely."

The reason, I reflected, was obvious. No matter how besotted she was about him, Althea must realize that he could not be trusted. Deprived long enough of drugs, an addict would betray anything or anybody.

"But she was sure that this other idea would work. You see, she'd found out something, something someone would be willing to pay out a good deal of money to have kept quiet."

Blackmail, then. I tried to keep my voice even. "Someone?"

"All she told me was that she'd found out something about someone who'd once been called Johnny the Boot."

Where had I heard that nickname? Frantically I searched my memory. Then I had it. One of those worn paperback books of hers had dealt with criminals of the nineteen-twenties. A chapter had been missing from it, a chapter listed on the table of contents page as "Johnny the Boot." I had assumed that the glue binding that chapter to the rest of the book had given way. But now I realized that Althea must have torn it out. Why? To confront someone with it?

Fear set my heart to pounding. If Althea had tried to blackmail some criminal — I said, "Are you sure that's all she told you?"

He sniffed again and moved nervously on the settee, crossing his legs and then uncrossing them. "That's all."

"And then she went away to close some sort of deal —"

"No, not then. First she took this quick trip to the States to see her grandparents. She said there were some details she had to check to make sure her idea would really work."

I stared at him, stunned and incredulous. How could my grandparents, that quiet, elderly pair in that little upstate town, know anything at all about someone named Johnny the Boot?

I said, "Are you sure?"

"Of course I'm sure. She flew there early last April. Two nights after she left she phoned me from her grandparents, just to say she was flying back to Milan the next day. When she got here, she said that everything had checked out, and that she was going away somewhere — I've no idea where — and cinch the deal. Except for the phone call she made from the railroad station, that was the last I've heard from her."

"The railroad station?"

"Yes. She said she'd almost collided with a truck, and now she felt too nervous to drive. She was going to leave her car near the station and take the train."

So that was how it was that the police had found her car there. I said, "Have you tried to get in touch with her?"

"Oh, sure. When she'd been gone more than a week, I wrote to her at her farmhouse. I thought she might have stopped by there before she came back here, or that maybe if she'd known she might be away for quite a while she had left a forwarding address. But she didn't answer, and my letter wasn't returned to me."

He had written to her once, and let it go at that. I said, "Do you happen to have a photograph of Althea?"

"Photograph? Oh, I understand. You haven't seen her for quite a few years, have you? You want to know what she looks like now."

He got up, walked over to a flimsy-looking desk of blond wood, opened its drawer, and brought back a large photograph with a lucite frame. As soon as he handed it to me, a faint hope died — a hope that somehow it was not my sister, but some other woman, who had been destroying herself in a vain effort to save a handsome weakling. The woman in the photograph, smiling over her shoulder, was Althea all right — older now, but still beautiful. Across the lower right-hand corner she had written, "For Freddie, with all my love, always. Althea."

As I silently handed it back to him, I wondered why he kept her picture hidden away. When he had restored it to the drawer and turned back to me, I asked, "Are you sure there is nothing more you can tell me?"

"I'm sure. As I said, Althea doesn't —"

The doorbell rang. Pale face alight with eagerness, he moved to the door and opened it. "Louisa! Come in."

A large, plain woman of forty-odd came into the room. He said, "Louisa, this is Maria, a new neighbor." The look he sent me held fervent appeal. "She just dropped in for a minute to say hello."

Her face unsmiling and suspicious, her fingers tightly gripping a large handbag of worn black leather, the woman nodded to me. Now I knew why Federico Scazzi had put away my sister's picture, and seemed so little perturbed by her absence. He had found a replacement for Althea, another woman to coddle him and keep him supplied with drugs — because that was what she carried, I felt sure, in that handbag he eyed so avidly. I wondered where he and this Louisa had met. Perhaps she was a nurse in a sanitarium where he had been a patient. She looked like some professional woman who had worked hard, saved her money, and now, in her middle years, found herself so lonely that she was willing to spend her savings on the likes of Federico Scazzi. No doubt she told herself, just as Althea had, that aided by her he would someday conquer his addiction.

He said to me, "Thanks for dropping in, Maria." His tone held a forced brightness. "Perhaps you can stay longer another time."

Too heartsick even to feel hatred for him, I said, "Yes, another time."

I walked past him and the woman and went out into the hall.

15

I drove across several intersections and then turned down a quiet residential street and parked at the curb. I thought of Althea's photograph with its loving inscription thrust away in that desk drawer. And I put my hands up to my face and wept.

After a while I took out a handkerchief and mirror and repaired the damage as best I could. Then I made a U-turn, drove back to the wider street, and started looking for an outdoor phone booth. When I found one, I looked in the phone book's advertising section for the Milan address of the airline from which I had bought my round-trip ticket. Then I drove on.

When I reached the airline office, I learned that there were vacant seats on a plane which, leaving Milan a little after five o'clock, would reach New York in the early evening. "You will be driving to the airport?" the ticket clerk asked.

"Yes."

He glanced at the clock. "You should have plenty of time to get there."

I hesitated, and then made my decision.

"All right. Please book me for the five o'clock flight." The sooner I saw my grandparents, the sooner I could return to Italy — armed with the knowledge of whatever it was they had told Althea.

The clerk handed my ticket back to me. I put it in my shoulder bag and then, from the bag's side pocket, took out the slip of paper bearing Jeffrey's telephone number. In one of the row of phone booths along the wall I dropped a coin in the slot, dialed, and then at the operator's direction, dropped more coins. Jeffrey answered the phone so promptly that I knew he must be seated at his desk.

"Could you keep Caesar for several days?"

His voice was sharp. "Why?"

"I'm flying to New York this afternoon."

"This afternoon!"

"Yes. I decided to call my grandparents and I learned my grandmother isn't well. There's room on the five o'clock plane, so I'm going to make a quick trip to Oak Corners."

"I see." After a moment he asked, "Did you find out anything more from the police, or at the railroad station?"

I was so tired and distraught that it took me several seconds to recall that I'd told him I intended to question the Milan police and the ticket sellers at the station. "No," I said, "you were right. I wasn't able to learn anything more."

Again he was silent for several seconds. Then he asked, "Are you sure? You sound very upset. Is it just because of your grandmother?"

"It is. Jeffrey, if I don't leave for the airport now, I'll miss my plane. Thanks for keeping Caesar," I said, and hung up.

A little after ten that evening, New York time, I opened the street door of my apartment house and went down the steps to my basement apartment. After I had unlocked my door and reached inside to switch on the light, I stood there for a few moments, feeling a dreamlike sense of unreality — not because my apartment had changed, but because it had *not* changed.

So very much had happened to me since I had last seen this room. Disjointed memories of the last ten days tumbled through my tired mind. The residents of that hilltop village, faces hostile in the reddish sunset light. Arturo in that Florence shop, showing me how to load and unload a revolver. Jeffrey Hale, features indistinct in the stairwell's dimness, looking up at me my first afternoon at the farm and saying,

"Who the devil are *you?*" That bronze figure holding its ancient symbols and smiling its strange smile. And then, only hours ago, Signora Bellini in her ornate salon, and Federico Scazzi shifting nervously about on the cheap settee as he said, "Althea doesn't confide in me completely."

All those people, all those events crowding into my life these past ten days. It was illogical, of course, but I felt it was strange that this room should look the same. It did, though. On the coffee table, lying face down, was the paperback novel I had been reading when the Contessa Rafaello phoned me. From the apartment of my hard-of-hearing neighbor directly overhead there came, as on any other Wednesday night, the sound of a situation comedy turned to full volume.

I locked my apartment door from the inside, went into the tiny kitchen, and measured coffee into the basket of a two-cup percolator. I was not hungry, even though I had eaten almost nothing on the plane. After a few mouthfuls from my dinner tray, I had turned and stared down through the window at the undulating sea of clouds below. Who was he, that man with the strange nickname, that man who, inexplicable as it seemed, was in some way connected with that gentle pair, my grandparents? I had kept asking myself that question throughout the flight and my bus ride at Kennedy to the long-term parking lot where I had left my three-year-old Audi.

Now, as I carried my coffee into the living room and sat down beside the phone, I was still asking myself that question. If this Johnny the Boot was a contemporary of my grandparents, someone they had known during their early days of marriage in the Bronx, then he must be in his late seventies now, or older. I thought of the elderly men I had encountered during those days in Italy. There had been Michele Rafaello, flushing with rage when I mentioned my date with his grandson. There had been a number of old men in that hilltop village, including the one who had called Althea a harlot. There was Domenico, the Giant fan. Come to think of it, there had been an old man asleep in the ornate salon of that house in Milan, a man Signora Bellini had addressed as "Father" —

But I realized that Johnny the Boot need not be one of those men. I had been in Italy ten days. My sister had been there more than seven years. In that time, she must have become acquainted with scores of men, including some "rich and prominent" man who patronized Signora Bellini's establishment, some man that Althea, in hope of blackmail, might have traveled to Rome to see, or Paris, or even Vienna.

I thrust the problem away from me. What I had to do now was to see my grandparents as soon as possible. Not that I expected that getting the truth out of them would be an easy task. They had not even told me of Althea's brief visit to Oak Corners last April. And when I phoned them with the news that I was going to Italy to see her, they had done their frantic best to stop me.

I knew that I would have a better chance of surprising the truth out of them if I descended upon them unannounced. But I could not do that. My grandmother had a slight heart condition. Best to give them a little warning.

I turned to the small table at the end of the couch, lifted the phone, and dialed that long-familiar number. After three rings, my grandmother answered. Apparently she had been expecting a call from some member of the other two Italian families in

Oak Corners, because she said, *"Buona sera."*

"Hello, Nana."

"Samantha! Oh, my darling," she said in Italian, "where are you?"

"In New York, in my apartment."

She turned slightly away from the phone. "Papa, Papa! It's Samantha. She's back!" Then, directly into the mouthpiece: "Are you all right?"

"Yes. I'm fine."

After a long pause she said, "And Althea? How is she?"

I already had decided what to do as soon as she asked that question. "I can't talk any longer now. There's someone at the door. But I'll drive up to see you tomorrow afternoon, and spend the night. 'Bye, Nana."

I hung up. For several minutes I just sat there. Even though this apartment looked the same, I was beginning to realize that it felt entirely different, and not just because Caesar was absent. It was as if I had brought with me some of the atmosphere of that old farmhouse, now standing again dark and deserted in the Tuscan night.

I carried my cup and saucer into the kitchen. It seemed to me that a long, long time had passed since, early that morning, I had started driving in my rented Simca to

Milan. I felt exhausted, and yet keyed up. I rinsed the cup and saucer and then went into the bathroom and began to run water into the tub, hoping that a warm bath would leave me sufficiently relaxed to sleep.

16

I awoke around ten the next morning with a groggy, disoriented feeling I knew must be jet lag. The day was both gray and steamily hot, which did not help my sense of malaise. Consequently I drove the Audi with especial care up the traffic-filled Hudson River Drive, and across the Harlem River and into the Bronx. Once I was out of the city and onto the Sawmill River Parkway, with the stream rushing foamy and cool-looking beside the road, I began to feel better. North of Poughkeepsie I left the highway for a series of narrow country roads that led past farms and apple orchards. Shortly after two I reached the first of the small houses built just outside the Oak Corners village line.

When I was a little girl, there was a big sign, erected by the Lions Club, at the edge of town. "Oak Corners, founded 1802," it said. "Watch Us Grow!" But like a lot of small towns in the northeast, it had not grown recently. In fact, after the small local shoe factory moved to Georgia — and cheaper southern labor — back in the nineteen-sixties, the town began to shrink. Many of the younger people moved away in search of jobs. Finally the Lions took their sign down.

Midway of the town's business district, I stopped before Ed's Candy Kitchen. As I drove north, I had reflected that those two elderly people I loved might try to deny that Althea had visited them in April, if indeed she had. After all, they had said nothing of such a visit when I phoned them just before I left for Italy. It was best that I find out from someone else if she had been here. Ed Saunders would know. There was scarcely a family in town who did not buy Ed's excellent homemade ice cream at least once a week. Consequently, he knew almost everything that went on.

The bell above the Candy Kitchen's screen door jangled as I went inside. Standing short and stout behind the counter, Ed beamed at me. "Samantha! I knew you'd be coming up here now that school's out. How've you been?"

"Fine. And you?"

"Can't complain. Seen your folks yet?"

"No. I thought I'd take them some ice cream."

He took down the topmost of a stack of quart containers and began to fill it with pistachio ice cream. Ed never asks his regular customers their flavor preferences. He remembers.

"Guess you know Althea was here — oh, early in April, I guess it was."

I nodded.

"She looked great. Althea's still the prettiest girl that ever grew up in this town."

"Yes." I paid him and carried the ice cream out to my car.

So there was no doubt now that she had been to see my grandparents. I drove down the tree-lined residential part of Main Street, past the fine old houses occupied by Oak Corners' leading citizens — the bank president, and the town's two doctors, and the founder of the shoe factory that had moved south. I passed, too, the white colonial house where my parents had lived and where Althea and I had been born. A retired couple from New York lived there now. Then I turned onto a street of smaller houses, and stopped in the driveway of the two-story green frame house where I had lived for all but the first eight months of my life.

As I climbed the steps, the front door opened and my grandparents came out. How small they both looked! My grandmother had always been little, and my grandfather, once a giant in my eyes, had shrunk with the years so that now he was only two or three inches taller than myself. Their lined faces held joy and thankfulness, but I read strain, even fear, in their dark eyes.

I set down the ice cream on the metal table in front of the glider swing, and hugged and kissed them both. After that we walked back to the kitchen, where I put the ice cream in the refrigerator, and then moved into the dining room. I don't know why, but at our house the dining room, not the living room, has always been the family gathering place. Even the TV is there, sitting on the sideboard.

We sat down at the round golden oak table. My grandmother asked, in Italian, "Did you have a good flight home?"

"Yes. It was very nice."

For a few seconds there was silence. Then she asked, "And did you and Althea have a good time?"

I could no longer put off telling them. "I didn't see her. She wasn't there."

Hopelessly poor dissimulators that they were, they made no effort to appear surprised. All I saw in their faces was an intensification of that fear.

"I didn't want to worry you," I said,

"and so I didn't tell you. But I knew even before I left New York that she was missing." I told them about the Contessa's phone call. "The Rafaellos thought she might have gone on a train trip somewhere. So did the police."

My grandfather seized upon that. "Sure. A trip. She will come back, or the police will find her. You stay here, Samantha. Don't go back there. Let the police find her."

Instead of answering, I sat silent, hoping that one or the other of them would say, "She was here last April." They did not. They just looked at me, their eyes pleading as well as frightened now.

Finally I said, "I hoped you might have some idea about what had happened. What did she say to you when she was here last April?"

It was my grandfather who answered. "Last April? What are you talking about, girl?"

"Please! I know she was here. Ed Saunders told me so." No need to tell them that a man named Federico Scazzi had told me first. Pray God they would never know Scazzi existed, or Francesca Bellini either.

My grandmother said, "Your sister

didn't want you to know she came to see us."

That seemed to be the case. She had gone back to Italy without even phoning me. But obviously my grandparents, too, had not wanted me to know of her visit.

"Why did she come here?" When they just looked at me, a pitiful stubbornness in their faces, I said, "She showed you something from an old paperback book, didn't she? A piece about someone called Johnny the Boot. She wanted more information about him. And she got it out of you, didn't she?"

My grandfather said in a blustering voice, "Are you crazy, girl? Why should Althea or anyone else ask us about this Johnny the Boot? What would your grandmother and I know about some criminal?"

I hated to point out that he had betrayed himself, but I had to. "If Althea didn't discuss him with you, how do you know what he was?"

My grandfather began to shout. For some reason — perhaps because he thought he would sound more forceful that way — he switched to English. "You lose-a your mind, girl? Look-a what you do to-a your grandmother! You want-a make her sick?"

199

I looked at her. The finely wrinkled face was white now, and her lips were shaking. I reached over and clasped her small, bony hand. "Oh, I'm sorry, I'm sorry. But if you talked to her, why won't you talk to me?"

Neither of them replied to that, but I felt that I could guess the answer. Althea must have had information that I did not. Perhaps she even remembered something from those years when I was still a small child, or perhaps not even born, something that made them realize that there was no use in trying to evade her.

I said pleadingly, "You love Althea, don't you? Won't you help me find out what has happened to her?"

My grandmother said, in Italian, "Of course we love Althea. But not like you. You came to us when you were a little baby. It was like — like raising your mother all over again."

She began to cry. I dropped to my knees and put my arms around her thin, sob-shaken body. Always I had been aware that my grandparents loved me best, not because I was more lovable than Althea, but because I had been in their care since before I could walk or talk.

She said brokenly, "Don't go back to

Italy. Let the police find out what — Oh, Samantha! If something happened to you, I'd want to die. Don't go back there."

"All right, I won't," I said, knowing full well that I would. I had to. Except for these two helpless old people, I was the only person in the world who loved Althea, or even gave a damn about what happened to her.

"You promise?"

"Yes." I got to my feet. "And we won't talk about this any more." After a moment I looked at my grandfather. "How is your garden this year?"

Vast relief in his face, he stood up. "Come. I will show you."

He and I went out to the back yard, where I admired the Italian broad beans, their tendrils already spiraling around the wooden poles he had set up for them, and the neat rows of pale lettuce, blossoming tomato plants, and feathery-topped carrots. The garden's soil, rich and dark because of the compost my grandfather had added for many years, appeared entirely free of weeds. As I often had of late years, I wondered how a man suffering from arthritis could keep such a fine garden.

Later on I helped my grandmother prepare a dinner of chicken cacciatore and zucchini. At the table we avoided all mention of Althea and Italy. Instead my grandparents talked of Oak Corners people I had known all my life, and I told them anecdotes about my students at that Manhattan school. Nevertheless, the atmosphere was strained, with frequent silences settling down, only to be broken by one of us speaking too swiftly and loudly. After dinner my grandmother washed the dishes, and my grandfather and I dried them.

Finally I said, spreading a dish towel on the rack, "Shall we play a little three-handed canasta?"

My grandmother said apologetically, "I'm just too tired, Samantha. I think I had better go to bed."

She looked tired. They both did. Probably they had not slept well after receiving my phone call the previous evening. I said, "I feel about ready for bed myself."

I went out to my car and took my small overnight bag from the trunk. Inside the house, I said good night to my grandfather, now in the dining room watching a TV game show, and then walked back to the ground-floor bedroom which my grandparents had occupied ever since the doctor had said that my grandmother should not climb stairs too often. I kissed her and then went up to the bedroom that had been mine as long as I could remember.

I turned on the light and looked at the four-poster single bed, its top sheet and blankets turned down at one corner, which my grandparents had allowed me to select when I became sixteen. The bed had been quite expensive. Despite their modest circumstances — my grandfather's watch repair shop had never made much — they somehow managed on occasion to be very generous with Althea and me. I looked at the kidney-shaped dressing table with its floral chintz skirt that matched the draperies, and the bookcase my grandfather made for me one Christmas, and my kneehole desk, with my dictionary and atlas still standing atop it between bookends. On impulse, I turned and crossed the hall to Althea's old room, opened the door, and switched on the light.

Althea, too, at the age of sixteen had been allowed to redecorate her room. She had chosen to have it done all in white except for touches of blue. I recalled how I, five years old at the time, had gazed with awe at my sister's transformed room. To me it had seemed a setting for a fairy-tale princess. Now, as I looked at the bed with its white organdy spread and white organdy canopy, at the photographs of William Holden and Rock Hudson on the wall, and at the crossed green and white pompons — she had been a cheerleader at Oak Corners High — near the photographs, I felt wonder that Althea had ever occupied a room so young-girlish.

On the white dressing table was a white telephone, my grandparents' gift to her on her seventeenth birthday. Later on, after Althea had moved to Manhattan, I used to come in this room and chat with my friends over the phone.

I lifted the phone from its cradle and listened. It was still connected. Perhaps my grandmother wanted an extension so that she would not have to rush downstairs if the phone rang while she was on this floor. Or perhaps — and this thought made my heart twist with pity — my grandparents left it connected out of some irrational hope that one or both of their granddaughters might come home, not just for a weekend now and then, but for good.

I replaced the phone in its cradle. Then, just as I started to reach for the light switch, I saw a tiny ball of crumpled paper lying between a rear leg of the dressing table and the wall. Evidently my grandmother, the last time she had set the room to rights, had missed seeing that bit of litter. I picked it up and smoothed it out on the dressing table. It was one of Althea's telephone doodles.

Her doodles were a family joke. Always we could tell to whom she had been talking on the phone, because invariably she would write down the name, sometimes accompanied by a sketch of the person, on the telephone pad. Often too there were phrases — bits of the conversation, or thoughts provoked by it.

Looking at the wrinkled sheet of paper, I was not surprised to see Federico Scazzi's handsome, ravaged face. Underneath it she had written, "Federico. Freddie. Freddie." Then below that: "Roots. Roots. Poisoned roots."

I looked at the small sheet of paper, feeling puzzlement and a strange inward shrinking. What thoughts had been going through her mind as she sat here three months ago talking to a man in Milan, her left hand holding the phone and her right hand busy with a pencil?

I tore the sheet into tiny bits and dropped it into the organdy-covered wastebasket. Back in my own room, I switched off the light and walked over to the window. For a long time I stood there in the darkness, inhaling the odor of green growing things, hearing the hard-shelled June bugs bump into the screen, and wishing I could turn time back to my teen-age years when I had so often stood here on summer nights, with no troubles except inconsequential ones, and no thoughts of my talented and beautiful sister except the proud, hopeful one that someday I would be with her in New York.

Finally I turned on the light, took Jane Austen's *Collected Novels* from the bookcase, and began to read myself into sleepiness.

17

In the morning my grandparents pleaded with me to stay at least one more day. Hating myself for the lie, I told them that I had arranged to give some of my pupils summer tutoring sessions starting the next week, and that I had to get back to my apartment to assemble the teaching materials I would use. I promised them that I would be back "soon" to spend several days with them, and I prayed that it was a promise I could keep. And of course I prayed, too, that I would not only find Althea, but be able to persuade her to leave Italy and come back to where her life had had its bright beginnings.

All the way to New York I kept reflecting that my trip to Oak Corners had been futile. Perhaps it would have been different if, before I flew back to the States, I had gone to the farmhouse and collected that mutilated paperback book. In New York I might have obtained another copy, one complete with the chapter on Johnny the Boot. Armed thus with additional knowledge, I might have gotten more facts out of my grandparents.

But I had been too eager to get to Oak Corners to even think of driving back to the farmhouse first. Besides, I probably could not have obtained another copy. I couldn't remember the name of the paperback publisher, but I knew it was not one I recognized. Probably that firm had gone out of business years and years ago.

Would it do any good to search through microfilmed back copies of *The New York Times*? No, because I had no idea of what the man's real name was. I did not know what the years were when he figured in the news, if he had. I might spend weeks or even months glued to the eyepiece of that microfilm viewer and still not find what I sought.

I already had reached the Hudson River Drive when I suddenly thought of Dr. Crownfield.

Laurence Crownfield, my sociology prof at N.Y.U., was a trivia buff. In fact, while still working for his Ph.D., he had been an instructor in the Department of Popular Culture at an Ohio university. His mind was like an attic stuffed with Americana. The names of all the actors who had played Tarzan on the screen. The name of Little Orphan Annie's dog. The title of every song that had won an Academy Award. Something of a showboater, he had liked to invite his classes at N.Y.U. to try to stump him with questions about the make of the car that had won the Indianapolis "500" in 1950, or Judy Garland's real name.

If anyone could furnish me quickly with information about someone nicknamed Johnny the Boot, Laurence Crownfield could.

I was lucky enough to find a parking space within half a block of my apartment house. As soon as I entered my living room, I looked in the Manhattan phone book. Fortunately only one Laurence Crownfield was listed. But when I dialed the number, there was no answer.

Could it be that he was teaching classes at N.Y.U.'s summer session? I called the university, and was finally connected with a girl who responded, "Dr. Crownfield's office." He was in class, she told me, but if I would leave my name and number, he would call me sometime within the next hour.

I hung up, and then called the airline. There were seats on tonight's flight to Milan, a clerk told me. Otherwise I would have to wait until Monday, because all weekend flights were fully booked. I hesitated, and then reserved a seat on that night's plane.

Minutes later the phone rang. "Miss Develin? Laurence Crownfield here."

"Hello, Dr. Crownfield. Perhaps you don't remember me, but I was in your —"

"Of course I remember you. Since I seat my classes alphabetically, you were in the front row. Small, quiet girl. Blondish. Good legs. Fairly good mind, too. Didn't I give you an A?"

"You did."

"What can I do for you now?"

"Could I see you sometime today?"

"Why not? I'll be in my office from two until three."

I thanked him, and hung up. On my way down to N.Y.U. I would have to stop at the bank and convert more of my savings into traveler's checks. I shuddered at the thought of the money I was spending, but there was no help for it.

Shortly after two that afternoon, Laurence Crownfield smiled across his desk at me. He was a thin, fortyish man with curly brown hair and brown eyes that often seemed to smile through his horn-rimmed glasses even when the rest of his face was sober. "Well, Samantha Develin, what is this all about?"

"Do you know anything about someone whose nickname was Johnny the Boot?"

"What is this? Are you trying to win a bet with someone?"

"No. It's more — serious than that."

The smiling look left his eyes. "I can see it is." Tilting his swivel chair back, he clasped his hands behind his head. "Johnny the Boot, Johnny the Boot. I've got it. Italian-born mobster back in the early twenties. Real name, Giovanni Something-or-other. Not one of the Chicago boys. New York. The Bronx, to be exact. In fact, he worked with the Donelli brothers. Protection and loan shark rackets. And bootlegging, of course." He smiled at me. "How am I doing?"

"Very well, of course. But if you can remember more —"

"I can, because his was an unusual case. He had a falling-out with the Donellis, and they tried to gun him down while he was walking along the street with his wife. They missed him completely but killed the woman. As far as I know from my reading about gang wars of that time, that was the only instance where gunmen made such a mistake.

"This happened in nineteen twenty-three or twenty-four. Johnny was under indictment at that time for income tax evasion. That's the charge the government used in those days when it couldn't nail mobsters for extortion or murder or Volstead Act violation. With his wife dead, I guess Johnny decided not to stay and fight the charge, but just slip out of the country."

"You mean he went back to Italy?"

"I imagine so. It would have been easy enough to bribe a freighter captain to give him passage, and then have him rowed ashore at some isolated spot on the Italian coast."

"But you can't remember his real name?"

He looked annoyed, although I couldn't tell whether it was with me for asking the question or himself for not knowing the answer. "It was something like Basquelli, but not quite that. Bostello? No, that wasn't it either, although it began with a 'B.' I'm sure I can look it up."

I thought of a shadowy living room in a house in Milan, and a handsome, cold-faced woman bending over an old man in an armchair. "Could it have been Bellini?"

"Perhaps. I'm just not sure."

"Do you know why he had that nickname? Could — could he have been a jockey at one time, say, or a shoemaker?"

"I suppose so. Or 'boot' could have been

short for bootlegger. Maybe I can look that up too. I've stored most of my files at my sister's place in Westchester. I'm going up there tomorrow morning for the weekend. I'll look up any information I have, and phone you."

"I'm afraid you won't be able to. I'm flying to Milan tonight."

"Tonight!" His gaze sharpened. After a moment he asked, "What airline?"

I told him. "Will you send me an airmail letter with the information? If you sent it tomorrow, I might get it by Monday or Tuesday."

He pushed a pencil and a pad of paper across the desk. "Write down the address."

A minute or so later I got to my feet. "Thank you very much, Dr. Crownfield."

He too stood up. His eyes weren't smiling at all now. "Wouldn't you like to tell me what this is all about?"

"I'm sorry, but no."

"Are you in some sort of trouble?"

He was a much nicer man than I had realized when I sat in his classes. His face held genuine worry now.

"I'm sorry," I repeated, "especially since you have been so helpful. But I can't talk about it. Good-bye, Dr. Crownfield. And thank you again."

18

Something went wrong with the hydraulic system of the plane assigned to that night's Milan flight. We passengers were kept waiting in the lounge for an hour past takeoff time. After we boarded the plane, there was another long delay. Finally we were transferred to a second plane which finally did take off, more than two hours late. The stewardesses, trying to soothe ruffled feelings, began to pass out free drinks and just-off-the-press copies of the next day's *New York Times.* I glanced at the date on my copy. July 10. Something was supposed to happen on July 10. What was it? Finally I remembered. That postcard Arturo Rafaello had sent me from Rome. It had said that he was returning to Florence in time for his sister's July 10 wedding.

I had not expected to have much appetite. But by the time the stewardess finally placed a plastic dinner tray before me, I was so hungry that I ate all of my overdone roast beef, most of my underdone frozen lima beans, and even several forkfuls of dessert, a soggy apple tart.

I also had expected to be wakeful. But apparently the accumulated fatigue of the past few days outweighed even my anxiety. When the stewardess had taken my dinner tray away, I walked back to a set of four-across empty seats at the rear of the plane, took a blanket and pillow down from the overhead locker, and stretched out. Almost immediately I fell asleep. Several times in the night a rough patch of air, or the voices of passengers moving along the aisle, aroused me briefly. But I did not come fully awake until the pilot, speaking over the intercom, wished us good morning and told us that it was raining in Milan.

A stewardess brought me a moist hot towel for my face and hands, and then orange juice, coffee, and Danish pastry. When she returned for my empty tray, she said, "Miss Develin, the co-captain tells me he received a message for you during the night."

My heart gave a frightened leap. Had something happened to my grandmother? Then I remembered that my grandparents did not know I was aboard this plane, or any plane.

The stewardess reached into her apron pocket and then handed me a slip of paper. "You're to call a Dr. Crownfield at this number any time after six this morning, New York time. That would be noon Milan time, of course."

Why had he chosen this means of communication, rather than writing me an air-mail letter? Remembering that worried look in his eyes, I realized he must have felt that the sooner he gave me whatever information he could, the better chance I would have of coping with whatever problem I faced. I thanked the stewardess, glanced at the phone number — a Westchester one — and put the slip of paper in my shoulder bag.

Because of that late departure from New York, plus head winds encountered during the night, the plane was more than three hours behind schedule when it slanted down through dark clouds and slashing rain to the runway at Milan. Thus it was not until almost one in the afternoon that I was through customs and able to ask the woman operator at the overseas telephone desk to put through a call to Laurence Crownfield.

When the operator reached the Westchester number, Dr. Crownfield answered so quickly that I was sure he had been hovering around the phone to catch it on the first ring, lest his sister's still-sleeping household be disturbed.

I said, "It's Samantha Develin, Dr. Crownfield. You wanted to talk to me?"

"Yes. I could tell yesterday that the answers to the questions you asked were damned important to you, for one reason or another, and so I drove up here to my sister's last night instead of today. Oh, hell, I might as well admit that wasn't my only reason. Not knowing the answers really bugged me. But anyway, I've got them now." He paused. "Johnny the Boot's real name was Giovanni Bortolino. Does that name mean anything to you?"

"No, nothing at all."

"Well, maybe the rest of my information will. None of the clippings in my file say exactly where he was born, but it was probably someplace in southern Italy. He entered this country illegally in nineteen nineteen, at the age of twenty. By the time he was indicted for income tax evasion five years later, he'd been arrested — but never convicted — for half a dozen crimes, including murder.

"As I told you, he was out on bail when his wife was killed. What I did not remember yesterday was that he had a child as well as a wife, a two-year-old daughter. Before Johnny skipped the country, he had her legally adopted by a Bronx couple. Respectable people, shopkeepers. Maybe he paid them well. Or maybe he'd done them favors in the past — let them off from paying protection money, for instance. All I'm sure of is that the adoption proceedings made the newspapers."

I could hear an odd ringing in my ears. It blended with the airport sounds coming muted through the phone booth's glass door — hundreds of voices and the shuffle of footsteps over marble and the blare of loudspeakers.

Nineteen twenty-four, I thought, with my damp hand gripping the receiver. That was not only the year a racketeer named Johnny the Boot had fled the country. It was also the year when a young Bronx couple named Luigi and Rosa Rossi had moved to Oak Corners, bringing with them enough money to buy a comfortable house and open a watch repair shop. They had also brought with them a two-year-old child, a girl who had grown up to marry a young lawyer named Donald Develin, and to give birth to Althea and Samantha Develin, and finally with her husband, plunge to her death in an out-of-control sports car.

Had my mother ever known the truth? I

felt sure she had not. But somehow Althea had been almost certain of the truth, or else she would not have flown the Atlantic to get final confirmation from that Oak Corners couple. Feeling my stomach tighten into a sick knot, I recalled the words written on that crumpled bit of paper I'd found in her room. I understood those words now.

Laurence Crownfield said, "The name of the couple who adopted Giovanni Bortolino's kid was Rossi — Luigi and Rosa Rossi."

I almost answered, "I know." Instead I asked, "Do you know now how he got his nickname?"

"Lord! I almost forgot that point. Yes, I was able to find it in an old true-crime pulp magazine in my files. It wasn't for any of the reasons you and I thought of. It was because he was born with a left leg nearly two inches shorter than his right. So that he would not appear crippled, he wore what is called a surgical boot — you know, a shoe with a built-up sole. Hence the nickname."

I stood motionless and silent in the hot booth. In my mind's eye I was seeing an old man walking slowly but normally along the terrace outside the Rafaellos' spacious salon. And I was seeing that same old man slip on the swimming pool's coping and then, face contorted with anger, taking a limping step or two toward me. I had assumed that he had hurt his foot when he slipped. I realized now, though, that his had not been the gingerly step of someone afraid to rest his full weight on an injured foot. The lurch in his walk had been much more pronounced.

Giovanni Bortolino, alias Johnny the Boot, alias Michele Rafaello. Giovanni Bortolino, Althea's grandfather — and mine.

Laurence Crownfield said, "Are you still there?"

It was hard to form the words. "Yes. But I had best get my car from the parking lot now. Good-bye, and thank you very much." I hung up.

19

Today, a Saturday, there were fewer trucks on the autostrada than there had been the Wednesday before. Noncommercial traffic was heavy, though, and because of the falling rain the endless lines of passenger cars, motorcycles, and holiday caravans moved at less than the usual suicidal Italian speed. As I drove the rented Simca, I kept glancing at my watch. If I remembered correctly, the Contessa had said that the time of the wedding ceremony had been shifted from eleven in the morning to four in the afternoon. If it was still set for four, I had a good chance of getting to the villa long before the reception, to be held at a "family friend's" house on the other side of Florence, was over.

I prayed, too, that the Contessa's father-in-law, who found "meeting people a terrible strain," had not joined those hundreds of wedding guests, but had remained at the villa. Probably he had. Probably, too, most of the family retainers had gone to the wedding.

No matter how strong and ruthless Giovanni Bortolino once had been, he was a frail old man now. Surely if I found him alone I would be more than a match for him. Surely, I thought, gripping the wheel hard, I could force him to tell me what had happened to my sister.

Although the rain stopped while I was still a few miles north of Bologna, there was ample evidence that while it lasted it had been far heavier here than around Milan. Water stood in roadside declivities, and evidently farmers had given up working the rain-soaked clay of the fields, because I saw no tractors, let alone ox-drawn carts and cultivators. My nerves stretched even tighter with the thought of the flooded roads I might find once I left the autostrada.

The feeder road gave me no trouble. It was after I turned onto a narrower road that I came to a puddle so large that it amounted to a small pond. Praying that afterwards I would not find my brakes useless, I inched my way through.

My brakes, as I learned by testing them a minute or so later, had not been affected. But soon I realized that something else had been. The engine had lost its smooth rhythm, and lost power too. Even with the accelerator down to the floorboard, the car moved at only a little more than forty miles an hour. It was obvious that despite my careful crossing of that puddle, the distributor head had become wet. I told myself not to panic. Forty miles an hour would be good enough.

I turned onto the still-narrower road that led to the farmhouse. Sunlight now beat down from a cloudless sky, so that the road and the fields steamed. I looked at my watch. A minute past four.

When I reached the farmyard, I saw that it looked fairly dry. Nevertheless I left my car up on the road, afraid that if I drove in I would become mired down. Since I was afraid, too, that I might not be able to start the engine again, I did not turn it off.

I hurried up the stairs, unlocked the heavy door. I had closed all the windows before I left Wednesday morning. Now the big room was smotheringly hot. I was aware of something else, too, something I had seemed to feel my first afternoon in this place — a sense of a silent vibration in the air, like a memory trace of something that had happened here. The atmosphere seemed thick with it.

Whatever the source of that feeling, whether a psychic echo of some terrible event or only my own overwrought nerves, I must not let it impede me now. I moved into the bedroom and opened the drawer of the stand beside the bed. The small gun Arturo Rafaello had enabled me to buy was still there, and still loaded.

With the gun in my shoulder bag, I moved back through those hot, silent rooms, relocked the door, and descended the stairs. When I was behind the Simca's wheel, I hesitated for a moment. If I followed the route I knew to the villa, I would pass Domenico Pasquale's house. If either he or Jeffrey saw me, they would expect me to stop and talk, and I dared not let them delay me for even a few minutes. The hands of my watch already pointed to four-fifteen. Furthermore, if Jeffrey gained an inkling that I was about to do something dangerous, he would try to stop me.

Should I try another route then? No, I might get lost. Best to take a chance and go past that other old farmhouse. I drove out of the yard and turned left. As I neared Domenico's house, I saw with relief that there was no one in the yard.

Seconds after I passed the house, though, I saw Domenico. He shuffled toward me along the roadside. At sight of the Simca he stopped, hesitated, and then, apparently sure of my identity, took off his battered hat and waved. Not stopping, I returned his wave as I passed him. At the rough marble bulk of the war memorial, I turned left and drove toward that villa halfway up the distant hillside.

Did Arturo know the past of the owner of that villa, and that Althea had tried to blackmail him because of it? I did not think so. Otherwise Arturo would not have welcomed me so cordially, and taken me out. Above all, he would not have helped me buy that gun. Nor could the Contessa know her father-in-law's identity, nor that Althea had threatened to reveal it. Otherwise the last thing she would have done would be to summon Althea's sister to Italy.

I moved up the long drive between the twin rows of cypress and stopped between the fountain and the flight of shallow marble steps. No sound came from beyond the balconied windows, closed and with blinds drawn against the afternoon sunlight. I had the distinct, and hopeful, impression that the place was almost deserted. Probably only one or two servants had been left to care for the Contessa's aged father-in-law.

I got out, climbed the steps, pushed the button beside the double glass doors with their protective wrought-iron grilles. After a few moments one of the doors opened. The uniformed maid who stood there was short, swarthy, and about eighteen years old. With relief I saw that my hopes had been justified. Even the elderly majordomo must have gone to the wedding.

I replied to the girl's greeting and then asked, "Is the Contessa at home?"

"Oh, no, signorina. All the family are at Signorina Sophia's wedding, and all the servants too except me."

My nerves tightened with alarm. "All the family?"

"Yes, except Signor Michele Rafaello."

"Where is he? In the swimming pool?"

"No, on the terrace. But, signorina —"

"Thank you." I brushed past her. With the protesting girl in my wake, I crossed the marble-floored entrance hall and the big salon, and moved through open doors onto the terrace. Back turned, dressed even in the heat in a black jacket and trousers, the old man stood at the balustrade.

The maid had followed me from the salon. "Oh, Signor Rafaello! I tried to stop her!"

He turned. I saw the mingled alarm and anger leap into his face. He said to the maid, "That's enough, girl. Leave us."

I heard her retreating footsteps. Then he

said in a low, angry voice, "So you are still here."

I too kept my voice low. "Yes."

"You fool! You utter young fool."

"Perhaps. But I'm not leaving this house until you tell me what happened to my sister."

His face flushed. "How should I know? Anything might have happened to a loose-living woman like that."

"Please!" I said. "There's no use in your evading. Althea found out who you are. That's why — whatever happened to her did happen."

He looked at me silently, the color draining from his face. I went on, "I know about you too now. I know about your years in New York, and your wife's death, and — and your little girl's adoption."

After a moment he said in an expressionless voice, "All right. This way." As he moved past me into the salon, I looked down at his right shoe. Its sole and heel were several times as thick as that of his left shoe.

He led me into the room from which Sophia Rafaello, accompanied by her princely fiancé, had emerged into the salon the first day I visited the villa. With the draperies drawn against the lowering sun, the light was so dim that I could barely make out that the room was a small library, furnished with a long heavy table and several straight chairs upholstered in leather. Floor-to-ceiling bookshelves lined the walls. Instead of opening the draperies, he turned on a tall, green-shaded lamp standing on the table. "Sit down."

We sat across from each other in the dimness, separated by the pool of light on the table's polished surface. I voiced the thought I had kept shying away from all during the drive from the Milan airport.

"You're my grandfather, aren't you?" Not Luigi Rossi, the gentle watch repairer and amateur gardener, but this massive-headed old man, gnarled hands trembling slightly as they lay on the table, and anger and fear plain in the dark eyes beneath the bushy brows.

He said, "What do you want of me? Money?"

I said coldly, "No."

"Your sister did."

"I don't. All I want is to learn what happened to Althea." When he did not answer, I forced myself to say, "Is my sister dead?"

A flicker of something in his eyes. Guilt? Pain? "I don't know. If you're sensible, you'll just go home and try to forget her."

I ignored that. "If she is dead, how did it happen?"

"I can't tell you that."

"Can't, or won't?"

"I can't, not for sure."

I believed him. I'm not certain why. Perhaps it was because that, no matter what evil he had done in the past, and no matter how harshly he spoke of Althea now, I could not believe that he had wanted to bring about his own granddaughter's death, either directly or indirectly.

I said, "Will you tell me as much as you do know?"

Instead of answering, he turned his face toward the small fireplace at one end of the room. On its mantel of dark marble stood a gilded clock. "Can you tell me the time? My eyes —"

"It is four minutes after five."

"Then we should have time to talk. All right, I will make a bargain with you. I will tell you about your sister, if you will promise me that afterwards you will go away, and stay away."

I said slowly, "You mean leave Italy? How can I promise that, when I don't know what you are going to tell me?"

The deep-set eyes studied my face. "I would have said that you are very unlike

229

your sister. But you do have one thing in common, a hardheaded stubbornness. All right, don't make any promises. I will tell you anyway, because I think that once I have, you yourself will see that there is nothing you can do here."

For a moment there was no sound in the room except the ticking of the clock. Then he said, "If you think that, just because you are my granddaughter, I am going to try to justify to you my years in New York, you are mistaken. I feel no need to justify them. Men who have done more harm in the world than I ever did are rewarded in all sorts of ways — medals, and high social position, and public office. But I do want you to know that I loved that child who grew up to become your mother. That was why I persuaded the best people I knew to adopt her."

I said, past a tightness in my throat, "How is it that you knew my — How is it that you knew the Rossis?"

"I was a boarder in their flat over the watch repair shop for a few months after I first came to New York. After I made a connection with the Donellis, of course, I was able to rent a fine big apartment of my own. I continued to see the Rossis, though. They knew I was in the rackets, but they still liked me."

He went on talking, his eyes fixed on my face, the tremor of his gnarled hands more pronounced at times. When he slipped out of the United States, he had not returned to his birthplace, Sicily. Instead, as Michele Rafaello, he had spent a few years in Naples, using the money he had brought with him from America to make even more money in the wine business.

"All those years I kept remembering what the Rossis had told me about the country around Florence — the beautiful hills and fields and vineyards and fine houses. Finally I came up here, looked at several villas that were for sale, and bought this one."

Soon after that he had married his second wife, a fairly rich widow several years his senior. "She didn't live to see our son made a papal count. That happened only two years before his own death. But she did live until after our son was married and Arturo and Sophia were born."

His second family, of course, knew nothing of the first one — the wife gunned down in the street, the child growing up in a small American town. But he didn't forget his daughter. When he felt that a sufficient number of years had passed, and that he was sufficiently well-established in his new identity, he made the first of several trips to Oak Corners, and was introduced to his growing daughter as "Uncle Johnny," a family friend from the old country.

"I felt I might draw too much attention to myself if I went to her wedding to that young lawyer. But I did visit Oak Corners soon after they moved into their fine big house there, and I came back again when Althea was six years old. As you might expect from a child, she asked questions about my right shoe, and I told her it had that thick sole because I was born with one leg shorter than the other. I never expected her to grow up remembering a thing like that. She did, though —"

His voice trailed off. When he again spoke, it was about the car crash that took my parents' lives. "I was not able to attend the funeral. I was in the hospital at that time, recovering from a heart attack. And when I again was able to travel — well, I just didn't want to go back to that town where my daughter had lived and died, not even knowing she was my daughter. Besides, by that time I had two grandchildren here."

"You went on sending money, though.

You'd been sending money to Oak Corners all along, hadn't you?"

"How do you know that?"

"I just guessed." I thought of the little luxuries — Althea's all-white room, and the four-poster bed in my room, and the art lessons provided for Althea as soon as it became apparent that she was talented. Strange to think that we had owed those things to an old man living in a palatial villa on the other side of the Atlantic.

He said, "Until Althea moved into that farmhouse seven years ago, I didn't even know she was in Italy. Until then she had been staying at a pension in Florence. It was Arturo who asked his mother to rent her the place. By that time I had turned all business matters over to my daughter-in-law and grandson."

"How had Arturo and Althea met?"

"In Florence someplace. I suppose it was inevitable that those two would get together. He was only eighteen then, but like lots of Italian men of that age, he was already highly sophisticated. And she was beautiful, and loose-living."

His voice held distaste. Plainly he, a man who a half-century before must have broken most of the laws in the criminal code, was in sexual matters a strict upholder of the double standard.

I said, "You must have been worried when you learned that your daughter-in-law had rented the farm to Althea."

"Worried that Althea would recognize me? Of course not. She had been only six when she last saw me. True, there was this right shoe of mine. But I knew that even if she remembered it — well, there must be thousands of men in the world who wear one built-up shoe. I met her a few times while she and Arturo were having their affair, and I never saw any sign of recognition in her face. I felt sure that unless something happened to make her realize it, she would never guess that I'd ever had anything to do with Oak Corners or the Rossis."

He fell silent for a moment. Then he asked, "Do you know why it was that Althea became so money-hungry?"

I was sure that both Arturo and Jeffrey had heard rumors about Althea's frequent visits to Milan. But apparently this aged man, seldom venturing away from his villa, knew nothing of Signora Bellini or Federico Scazzi. And certainly I was not going to tell him.

"No," I said. "When did you realize that she wanted money?"

"When my grandson told me that she had come to him, offering to split fifty-fifty if he would help her sell this ancient statue she had found. I suppose she turned to him because she'd heard of a little trouble he'd been in over our vineyards near Rome."

"Trouble?"

He shrugged. "The government charged that he was selling adulterated wine as vintage. Arturo was not indicted. And even if he had been, the penalty would have been light. But stealing art treasures from the Italian government — ah, that is a very serious matter indeed. Arturo turned her down."

"Did she tell Arturo where she had found it?"

"No, of course not, not when he wouldn't go along with her scheme. Whether she approached anyone else, I don't know. Probably not, because it must have been only a few days later that she discovered a way to make a lot more money, or at least thought she had."

Not only his hands shook now. There was a tremble in his voice. "She came here one day last April. Came here just as you did, when she was quite sure the rest of the family would not be here. You were sure of that today, weren't you?"

"Yes. Your granddaughter's wedding —"

"The day Althea came here, she must have heard that my daughter-in-law and granddaughter were in Paris shopping for a trousseau. Arturo was at the bank, of course. Althea didn't even ring the doorbell. Instead she circled the house, saw me on the terrace, and climbed up to where I was sitting. She suggested we go down beside the swimming pool and talk. I, of course, had no desire to talk to her. Just knowing that a grandchild of mine had become a wanton was bad enough. But when I refused her, she said, 'Unless you want your servants to hear, Signor Bortolino, you had better do as I ask.' "

I thought of this frightened old man and my sister confronting each other on the sun-flooded terrace. Not the vivacious teenager I remembered from my childhood, or even the poised and beautiful young woman who, later on, had come up from New York every now and then to dazzle my high school friends. The Althea on the terrace that day had been older, a great deal harder, and utterly obsessed by her need to "save" an unsavable man in Milan.

"I went down to the swimming pool with her, of course. She showed me these printed pages she'd torn from a book. They were all about me, Johnny the Boot. My connection with the Donellis in New York, my indictment, the death of my wife, the adoption of my daughter by a watchmaker and his wife, who later moved to upstate New York. For some reason — perhaps some sort of delicacy — the author had not given the name of the couple who had adopted my daughter. But he had written enough to make her remember how, when she was six, an Italian 'Uncle Johnny' with a built-up shoe had visited Oak Corners, and been more than cordially received by the people she had always thought were her grandparents.

"She had flown back to New York to make absolutely sure she was right. I guess Luigi and Rosa, caught by surprise, had told her that yes, Giovanni Bortolino and Michele Rafaello were the same man. I imagine that later they were terrified at the thought of what she might try to do with the information, and what might happen to her. You see, I was their friend. They were grateful to me, and not just for small favors. They were grateful because through me they had had what otherwise they would not have had, a daughter and grandchildren. And yet they knew —"

He broke off, but I realized what he had been about to say. Those old people knew what he was, a criminal who had terrorized their neighbors, extorted money, and, if he had not actually murdered, had been an associate of those who had. No wonder that they had not looked surprised when I told them Althea was missing. And no wonder they had pleaded with me not to return to Italy.

I said, "What did Althea want from you?"

"Five hundred thousand dollars, American. In cash. Otherwise she would tell all she knew."

He leaned toward me. "Consider my position. She was my granddaughter. But she was a wanton, and a blackmailer. And she was threatening not just me. She had it in her power to destroy the position of my daughter-in-law, a contessa, and of my grandson, a banker, and of my granddaughter, who was about to become a princess."

I said, dry-mouthed, "And what did you do?"

"I told her that I would send a check by a servant to the bank, and bring her the money that night."

"And did you?"

"Of course not. Only a fool starts paying blackmail. It was Arturo who went to see her that night."

"You told him what she was threatening?"

"Yes. I told him everything, all the things about my past that he had not known before. I had to. I am an old man. I can no longer deal with danger. But I have Arturo. And I have always been aware that in a crisis I would find that he is far more of my blood than his father was."

I thought of the adulterated wine sold at vintage prices. Yes, Arturo was a far truer descendant of Johnny the Boot than that pious papal count could ever have been.

"Did you tell your daughter-in-law?"

"No, nor my granddaughter. A man does not bring his womenfolk into such matters. Although perhaps in this case — I mean, my daughter-in-law is a penny pincher. Perhaps Arturo and I should have foreseen that she would become worried about that unpaid rent, even to the extent of telephoning you. But we did not."

I moistened my lips. "You said Arturo went to see Althea. What did he say to her?"

"I don't know. I did not want to know. When he returned to the villa that night, he came to my room and told me that she would never bother us again. He said she was someplace where no one would ever find her."

That old farmhouse, and the sense I'd had more than once that the air between the thick walls vibrated with the memory of some terrible event. I said in a voice I would not have recognized as my own, "He killed her, didn't he?"

The gnarled old hands were shaking violently now. "If he did, I did not want that to happen. I wanted him just to — scare her off. But also if he did, you will never be able to prove it. You can't prove murder unless you produce a body, and I believe Arturo when he says no one will ever find her.

"Of course," he went on, "you can go to the police and tell them all I have just told you. Arturo and I will deny, of course, that either of us had anything to do with Althea's disappearance, and you will have no way of proving that we did. Still, you can reveal my former identity, and that would hurt my family terribly. I don't speak of myself. After all, I'm well past eighty. But I don't want them destroyed."

When I didn't answer, he went on, "And if you turn the spotlight on them, you'll be turning it on yourself and your sister, too."

The spotlight. I thought of reporters from Italy's scandalmongering newspapers and magazines, following up leads about Althea's frequent visits to Milan, and finding out about Federico Scazzi and Francesca Bellini. And I thought of the added suffering that would bring to those two old people in Oak Corners, blameless people who loved their adopted daughter and who, after her tragic death, had loved and tried to do their best for her two children.

"My grandson is clever and ruthless," he said. "Get far away from him, while you still can."

Arturo was clever all right, so clever that to forestall any suspicion I might have of him, he had actually helped me to acquire the pistol which now weighted my shoulder bag. And he had been clever enough to terrorize me by such childish means — the ignited oil drum, the crude crayon sketch — that I would be unlikely to connect such acts with the gallant young man who had taken me to dinner and kissed my hand in farewell.

In the silence the clock on the mantelpiece began to strike. He said, through the sound, "Is it six? Six o'clock already?"

"Yes." My heart gave a frightened leap.

"You mean that the others —"

"Yes! They may be on their way back here. Leave! Arturo must not find you here. He must not know you have even been here. If he does, he'll guess why. I'll tell the maid not to — Now go on. Go to Milan. Maybe you can catch an evening flight to New York."

I pushed back my chair. "All right," I said.

20

The sturdy-looking little maid was in the entrance hall, applying a feather duster to the marble statue of a Grecian nymph. I saw the curiosity in her dark gaze as we exchanged good-byes. Swiftly I went down the steps through the late afternoon light and got into the Simca.

Its engine would not start. I forced myself to wait a few moments, feeling the sweat spring out on my forehead and upper lip, and then tried again and again. After that I just sat there, hands gripping the wheel. If I could not start it soon, what should I do? Strike out across the fields toward Domenico Pasquale's house? That might be my best chance, even though Arturo would recognize the Simca when he saw it here, and guess that I was trying to get to Domenico's —

Footsteps. My head swung around. The plump maid was approaching the car. "The signore said I must push. Once you are around the fountain —"

I saw what she meant. Only a few feet ahead the drive, encircling the fountain, began to slope downward. My gaze quickly swept the villa's façade. No sign of anyone watching. But I knew he must be there somewhere, watching through a crack between drawn draperies.

I said, "Do you think you are strong enough to —"

"I am very strong. And the car is small."

I said in a shaking voice, "Then quickly, please."

The little car moved forward, inch by inch at first, and then faster as the slope of the drive increased. Before I turned onto the straight stretch leading down to the road, I waved my thanks to the maid.

Gaining speed with every second, the Simca moved down between the cypress. Still the engine did not start. Then, when I was only a few yards from the end of the drive, it sputtered into life. Weak with relief, I turned onto the road.

A little caravan of cars was moving toward me.

My foot lifted spasmodically from the accelerator. The Simca bucked and almost stalled. Then, hands tight on the wheel, I drove on. I could see that there were three cars, a fairly old sedan, a long limousine, and, bringing up the rear, Arturo's red Alfa Romeo. I passed the first of the cars. Servants in their Sunday best. The young footman I had seen down by the swimming pool was at the wheel. The chauffeured limousine carried three women, the Contessa and two who were strangers to me. All wore elaborately flowered hats. I caught the startled look on the Contessa's face as she nodded a reply to my wave.

Arturo was alone in the sports car. The face he swung toward me was pale, rigid. I stretched my lips into a smile that must have appeared like a grimace and then drove on, heart pounding with the conviction that he would make a U-turn and come after me. He did not. In the rear-view mirror I saw him speed up, pass the other two cars, and turn into the villa's drive.

I pressed hard on the accelerator. Only about three miles to that rough marble monument, and then another half mile to Domenico's farm and Jeffrey Hale. I could get there before he caught me. Surely I could. Anyway, I might meet another car soon. I would get out, hail it —

Foot down to the floorboard now, I drove on. No car approached along the narrow road. Then, in the rear-view mirror, I saw a flash of red as the Alfa Romeo emerged from between the twin rows of cypress and sped after me.

Even though I knew that the Simca had reached its top speed, my foot pressed down still harder. Ahead was a slight rise. Beyond it, I knew, I would see the monument, at the spot where this road joined the one leading past Domenico's house. If I could get even that far, perhaps I would encounter some traffic —

He caught me a few hundred yards short of the monument. The Alfa Romeo drew a little ahead of me and then angled toward my side of the road, blocking my way. Instinctively I trod on the brakes, and the engine stalled. I heard the other car's door slam, saw him striding toward me, tall and handsome in formal striped trousers and dark jacket. It was then, and not until then, that I remembered I had with me the gun he had helped me to acquire. My hand darted toward my shoulder bag, lying beside me on the seat.

"No!" he said sharply.

His right hand, holding a gun, rested on the sill of the car's door. I stared at that ugly little circle of steel. With his left hand he reached into my shoulder bag, took out the revolver, and dropped it into his coat pocket.

"You are to drive to the farmhouse now," he said.

Wordlessly I looked at him. Arturo Rafaello, young Florentine banker and, since sometime this afternoon, brother-in-law of a prince of ancient lineage. With weird detachment I reflected that he was also a relative of mine. A cousin? No, half-cousin. His father, the papal count, had been a half-brother to that little girl left long ago with a Bronx watchmaker and his wife.

"Start your engine. I'll pull over so you can drive ahead of me. But don't be foolish enough to speed up. You know you can't outrun me. Don't try anything at all. Just drive. Slowly."

My lips felt wooden. "There's something wrong with my car. I don't know whether I can start it again."

"Try it."

I tried. The motor caught.

As I drove ahead of the Alfa Romeo toward the monument, I wondered with desperate hope if he had forgotten that we would pass Domenico's house. If I could make a quick left-hand turn off the road and drive, horn blaring, into the yard, surely he would not dare —

But he had not forgotten. Almost as

soon as I had turned at the monument and seen Domenico's ocher-brick house up ahead, its yard empty, the red car drew level with me, forestalling any attempt I might make at a quick turn. Left hand on the wheel, an odd little smile on his lips, he lifted his other hand briefly so that I could see the gun. I drove on, aware that Domenico's house was behind us now, aware that unless we met another car I had lost my last chance to find help. He had killed my sister, that handsome man in the car keeping pace with mine — I had no doubt now that he had killed her — and if my own life was to be saved, I was the one who would have to do it.

I would talk to him, I decided desperately. I would promise him that if he would let me live I would fly back to New York this very night, if that was possible, and never tell anyone what I knew.

We had almost reached the farmhouse now. He speeded up and then, just beyond the entrance to the yard, angled the red car across the road, blocking my way. I turned and, aware that the Alfa Romeo followed, drove halfway into the yard and stopped.

I heard the door of his car open and close. On legs that shook I got out of the Simca and stood facing him. He still held the gun, but at his side now, his hand almost concealing it. His other hand held a large flashlight. If someone passed on the road now, they would see only a girl and a handsome, impeccably dressed man chatting in the sunset light.

I forced out words. "Please. Please tell me what this is all —"

"There is no use in your trying to pretend, Samantha. The maid tried to, but after I told her I had passed you on the road, she admitted that you had been there, shut up in the library with my grandfather for almost an hour. There is only one reason you could have come to the villa when you knew you almost certainly would find him alone, and there is only one topic you two could have discussed."

I seized upon that. "I told your father I would fly back to New York right away, and never tell anything I — I know. He believed my promise. Why can't you?"

"Because I am not like my grandfather, half senile."

I said, fighting to keep my voice calm, "Do you think you can get away with making two of us disappear within three months of one another?"

"Yes."

I remembered what the old man had said. No one can be charged with murder in the absence of a body.

"Anyway," he went on, "I know there is one thing I can't do. I can't risk your talking. Now turn around, Samantha, and walk through that grove of olive trees. I'll be right behind you."

Beneath my numb terror I felt surprise. I had expected him to order me up the stairs. Somehow I was sure that it was in those rooms that my sister had died. He had killed her there, and then cleaned up all evidence of his act, and then taken her under cover of darkness — where? Somewhere where no one would ever find her, he had told his grandfather.

"Go on, Samantha."

No use to scream. All a scream might do would be to bring a bullet crashing into me immediately. No use to run toward the road. The gun in his hand would cut me down before I could take even a few steps. I turned and, skirting the edge of the terrace, moved away through the grove.

The air was hotter among the olive trees, even though a faint wind moved their topmost branches. Aware that he was close behind me, I walked over ground on which shifting spots of reddish sunset light alternated with leaf shadows. My blood was pounding with the knowledge that at any moment a bullet could slam into the back of my neck and angle upward through my brain.

We emerged from the trees, began to climb the low hill. Still I had not felt it, that blinding explosion in the brain. We descended the hill. Then, in the long, still damp grass of the little valley, I came to an involuntary halt. I knew now where he was taking me.

I felt the gun prod me between the shoulder blades. "Go on. Why are you stopping?"

"The — the statue —"

He said sharply, "What statue? Turn around."

Like an automaton, I obeyed. "The one in the cave. The Etruscan goddess."

In the sunset light his face was dyed red, like those of the villagers that evening I had visited the walled town on the hill. "So you found it. Have you told anyone?"

Frantically I wondered whether yes or no would be the wiser answer. Then he smiled and said, "I can see that you haven't. Not that it matters much."

"When did you find it?"

"A few days after your sister came to me

with the crazy idea that I help her sell it illegally. She'd gone away by then to visit that American village of yours. I guessed the thing must be somewhere in the vicinity of the farmhouse, so I searched until I saw those old hand-hewn stones. After that it was easy."

"Are — are you going to sell it?"

"And risk imprisonment for a few hundred thousand lire? Of course not. Now go on, Samantha. Don't attempt that old trick of trying to keep me talking."

I stood motionless. In that reddish light his face looked stony, implacable, the skin drawn tight over the bones. He said, "I don't want to, but if I have to, I'll do it right here. Now turn around and go on."

I understood them then, all those people who, instead of putting up some sort of fight, have turned and, with a gun at their backs, walked with seeming meekness to their deaths. At least that way you gain a few more seconds of life. I turned and moved up the hill, through tall grass strewn with ancient stones, to that dense thicket of cypress.

It was almost dark there among the tall trees. Once I stumbled over something — an exposed root, one of those whitish stones? — and went down. "Get up," he said. I lay motionless. If he pocketed the flashlight and leaned over me to haul me to my feet, perhaps I could seize his hand that held the gun —

I felt a cold metal circle press against the back of my neck. "Get up." I struggled to my feet and went on, arms crossed before my face to ward off the lashing branches. Althea's face flashed before my inward vision. What had been her thoughts as she struggled through these same trees one night last April? And then I remembered that probably she had been already dead. I imagined him carrying her over his shoulder through the darkness, his head bent to ward off branches, the flashlight in his free hand directed down to underbrush and strewn stones.

I emerged onto the slanting lip of earth in front of the cavern. "Go on." I stepped over the low sill of crumbling rock into almost complete darkness and then stopped. The gun's mouth, hard between my shoulder blades, prodded me forward a step or two. Then the flashlight's glow bathed that smiling figure with ancient symbols of life and death in her hands.

The flashlight's beam left the statue, swept a few feet to the right, and then stopped at the narrow opening in the cavern's rear wall. "In there," he said.

"No!" I cried. And then, with no recollection of having moved, I found myself standing, back against the rocky wall, with scream after scream ripping from my throat.

The beam dazzling my eyes swept upward, so that for a split second I seemed to be in total darkness. Then the flashlight crashed against my left temple, sending a wave of pain through my head, staggering me so that I almost fell.

"Now go on." His voice, raised and angry, reverberated in that confined space. "Do as I say."

It seemed to me that through the painful ringing in my head, through his shouted words, I had heard another sound. Wild hope surging within me, I looked at the dimly visible figure beyond the flashlight's beam. Had he heard? Apparently not. His head had not turned.

"Go on. Move!"

Perhaps he had heard no sound because there had been none.

"All right." His voice was quiet now. I heard the click of the gun's released safety catch. "If that's the way it has to be —"

I turned then and moved through that narrow opening into air that was damper, cooler. The flashlight's beam, shining past me, illuminated a short passage and the rough opening of another cavern beyond.

I moved into the second cave and then halted. Only a few feet ahead of me a low, roughly circular coping of stones, obviously man-made, surrounded some sort of opening in the cave's floor. On the near side the coping was broken by a thin, whitish rock that lay flat on the ground. Through the ringing in my ears, through the pounding of my heartbeats, I could hear the sound of swift-running water.

Again the gun prodded my back. I moved forward to the coping's edge. The flashlight's beam was directed over my shoulder to the cavern's rocky rear wall, but by its refracted glow I could see the irregular opening, roughly four feet by five feet, in the cave's floor, and below it the gleam of black, rippling water. An underground stream.

Demeter in her infernal aspect, guardian of caves, and springs, and underground waters.

Something arched over my shoulder, struck the black water, sank. I knew it must have been that gun, registered to my name at police headquarters in Florence.

In the same way, Althea's body had gone

into that swift-flowing stream. And from there, where? To that river in the valley, to be wedged among rocks or ancient tree stumps on its bed? Or had she been carried to the Arno, swollen three months ago with melting Apennine snow, and from there swept into the sea?

The light shifted. I realized that to leave one hand free he had placed the flashlight on the cave's floor. "Kneel down," he said, "on that flat rock."

The sacrificial rock where more than two millenniums ago other creatures — animal? human? — had drawn the last few breaths of air into their lungs. Seconds after I knelt there, my lifeless body, with a bullet hole at the base of the brain, would topple neatly, cleanly into the black water and be swept away beyond almost any chance of recovery. There would be no blood, no signs of struggle. He could make his way back to the farmyard then, and drive in his sleek car to the villa, and wait serenely for the day when he would open his newspaper to read that some farmer, some wandering tourist, had chanced upon the Etruscan goddess and the sacrificial stone she guarded.

Through my terror rose a blinding rage. Not both of us, I thought. Not both of us!

I turned to face him and screamed, "No, no! You can't!"

A thunderous sound in the outer cavern, and the scrape of clawed feet running over a rocky surface. Arturo whirled around. Over his shoulder I saw, in the upward-striking light, the gleam of eyes and then the big, furry body hurtling from the narrow passageway.

Arturo fired. I heard Caesar's yelp of pain, almost like a human scream, mingling with my own scream. But the dog kept coming. Standing paralyzed, I saw him launch himself into the air. Arturo fired again.

Paralysis left me then. I saw the flashlight lying on the ground several feet away, and started toward it. Some protuberance on the cavern floor caught my toe, and I fell jarringly to hands and knees. Dizzy, head still throbbing from the blow I had received, I stayed there for a second or two, and then managed to get to my feet.

My blurred vision showed me that there were two men in the cave now, two men locked in struggle, their merged, elongated shadow moving crazily along the rocky walls. As I watched with dazed eyes, I heard the gun go off again. The shorter of the two men stepped back, his right fist looping upward. I caught a glimpse of Arturo's face as he staggered against the cavern wall, with the gun flying from his hand. I heard it strike something, turned my head in time to see it slither to the edge of that flat rock and then disappear into the liquid blackness below.

Numbly I turned my head and looked at the two men, again locked in struggle, feet scraping and slipping over the rocky floor. Then Arturo broke free. I caught a glimpse of his face, blood streaming from one nostril, before he turned and darted away down the passageway.

Jeffrey's brilliant eyes threw me one look. Then he too plunged down the passageway.

Half-fainting, I leaned against the rock wall. Silence now, except for my own ragged breath and the liquid sibilance of the underground stream. My gaze moved over the cavern floor. Blood, dark and glistening, there just inside the entrance from the passageway. Arturo's? Then, my heart contracting with grief, I remembered, and knew whose blood it was.

I bent and picked up the flashlight. A trail of Caesar's blood lay along the passage. I found him just inside the outer cave's rocky doorsill. Obeying his instincts, he must have tried to drag himself away so that he could die someplace down there among the trees on that steep slope, now barely visible in the twilight. But he had not made it.

For the first time I saw that his leash was attached to his collar. When he heard my first screams, and gave that one answering bark down there on the slope, he must have pulled free of Jeffrey's hand and scrambled the rest of the way to the cave.

I knelt beside him. His white chest was matted with blood. His brown eyes, always so full of life and intelligence, were glazed now. I lowered my ear to his side. No breath stirred the massive rib cage.

I began to cry then, my tears falling unchecked onto the thick fur. I wept for all that had happened. I wept for my beautiful, self-destructive sister, who had thrown away talent, and self-respect, and finally her life. I wept for those two frightened and sorrowing old people in Oak Corners. And I wept for the friend on whose furry body my cheek rested, my friend who never again would walk protectively beside me through Greenwich Village streets, or anywhere else.

I don't know how long I huddled there, head pillowed on his motionless body, dimly aware that beyond the glow of the flashlight in my hand there now was complete darkness. Finally I heard the sound of someone moving up the slope, and then Jeffrey's voice calling my name. Sitting up, I called an answer.

A few minutes later he stepped over the crumbling remains of the rock wall. Stooping, he took the flashlight from my hand, straightened, and shone its light on my face and Caesar's still body.

"We had best leave him here," he said quietly. "I'll come and get him in the morning."

I nodded. After a moment I was able to ask, "What happened to —"

"Best to get down to the farmhouse before I tell you. That's a bad bruise you have. We should put cold compresses on it."

"Please! I need to know now."

He said reluctantly, "I couldn't quite catch up with him. I got to the farmhouse in time to see him drive across the yard and turn left onto the road. I went after him in my car. By the time he reached the turnoff to the villa, we must both have been doing eighty. He couldn't make the turn. Instead he crashed into the monument."

"Is he —"

"There's no chance at all that he is alive. The whole front end of the car was smashed back in on him, like an accordion. I drove back to my place, phoned the carabinieri to say that there had been an accident, and then came here."

"Is that all you told them?"

"Yes. I said I'd heard the crash, and gone to investigate. I couldn't know whether or not you'd want me to say more than that, not until you'd told me what this is all about. Come on, now."

His hand drew me to my feet. Before I moved past Caesar into the night, I caught a glimpse of the bronze goddess, smiling as she had for perhaps twenty-eight hundred years, her small, mysterious, and chilling smile.

21

In the farmhouse half an hour later I lay on the bed. Except for a swath of lamplight shining from the kitchen, the room was in darkness. Jeffrey, sitting beside me on a straight chair, dipped a washcloth once more into the pan of cold water on the nightstand, wrung it out, and laid it against the left side of my face. "How does it feel now?"

"Most of the pain has gone. I don't think I need the compress any longer."

"All right." He took the cloth and dropped it into the pan of water. "Do you want to talk to me now?"

I nodded.

"Well?"

Scenes tumbled through my mind. Althea on Parents' Day at Oak Corners Grammar School, smiling her approval of the second grade's Halloween drawings posted along the hall, while I moved proudly beside her. Rosa Rossi, lips shaking as she said, "Of course we love Althea. But not like you." Caesar, perhaps already with one bullet through his heart, launching himself at the man with the gun —

Helplessly, I began to cry. Jeffrey said, "Move over." He lay down beside me, and pillowed my head on his shoulder. "Now tell me."

Still crying, and now and then skipping backward and forward in time, I told him. Signora Bellini. Federico Scazzi. How I'd hoped all through high school that someday I would join Althea in New York. My useless conversation two nights ago with those two old people I loved. My call to Dr. Crownfield from that phone booth at the Milan airport. Facing the old man once known as Johnny the Boot across the library table in that luxurious villa. My long, long walk with a gun at my back through the olive trees and up through the cypress grove.

When I finally stopped talking, he looked at the ceiling for several seconds, and then asked, "What do you want to do about him?"

I knew whom he meant. Arturo's grandfather — and mine.

"Nothing. He's an old man now. And the others, the Contessa and her daughter, they're innocent. And they'll be suffering enough over Arturo's death.

"Besides," I went on, "if — if we reveal

things about that old man, people might learn things about Althea too. That Federico Scazzi in Milan, and Signora Bellini. It's bad enough that I know those things. I don't want others to know, especially not my grandparents." To me those two would always be my grandparents.

"All right. Then Rafaello's death will remain just an accident. He tried to take a corner too fast, that's all."

It was not until then that I thought to ask, "How is it that you followed me up there tonight?"

Domenico, he told me, had reported to him that I had passed him on the road that afternoon, and then turned off at the monument. "I supposed you were going to Isolotta for some reason, and would be back soon, so while I was working at my desk, I kept looking out the window every now and then.

"Finally I saw your car and Rafaello's coming side-by-side down the road. I thought you were chatting as you drove along, the way people sometimes do on a country road. I kept waiting to see the Alfa Romeo drive back on its way to the villa, but it didn't, and — oh, hell, there's no point in saying I was worried. I wasn't, right then. But I was a little burned up at the idea of Rafaello being there so long, when you hadn't even stopped by to say hello to me since your return, so finally I put Caesar in the car and drove over here."

It was Caesar's strange behavior that first made him realize that something might be wrong. "Maybe dogs do have ESP. Anyway, he began barking as soon as we turned into the farmyard, and even before the car stopped, he leaped out and ran to the edge of the olive grove. He turned there, still barking, as if demanding that I come with him. Instead I went up the stairs. Caesar didn't follow me. He stayed down at the foot of the stairs, still barking. From that I knew, even before I knocked on the door and got no answer, that you weren't in the house. I ran down the stairs and put his leash on him."

Every now and then stopping to sniff at the ground, the shepherd had dragged Jeffrey through the olive trees and over the low hill beyond. "We were about halfway through that stand of cypress trees when you screamed. He gave one bark and pulled the leash out of my hand. I followed him as fast as I could."

I thought of Caesar lying up there near the foot of the smiling goddess. After several seconds I said, "That Etruscan figure.

I suppose you want the honor —"

"It's an honor I can do without. When I go up there for Caesar in the morning, I'll see if I can wipe out all traces of what happened there tonight. Dirt sprinkled over the floor of the cave might do it."

Dirt to cover the stains where a dog had bled to death.

"If when I've finished I think everything looks okay, I'll phone the Archaeological Museum, anonymously, and tell them where to look. Otherwise I'll let someone else find it."

After a moment he added, "Go to sleep now."

I must have been more exhausted than I realized, because I did go to sleep almost immediately. Sometime later his arm, easing out from under my head, aroused me briefly. I heard the wardrobe door creak open, felt him spread something light and warm — my terry-cloth robe? — over me, and then I went back to sleep. Sometime before morning I again awoke. The rustle of a magazine or book page turning in that lighted kitchen told me that he was still there.

The next time I awoke, sunlight was slanting into the room. From somewhere below came the sound of a shovel's scrape.

I got up from the bed and, dimly aware of my rumpled clothes and of a subdued ache in my left temple, went to the window. Jeffrey was invisible. But the scraping sound, I could tell now, came from the olive grove.

Hastily I washed my face, changed into jeans and a tee shirt, and went down the stairs. As I entered the grove, Jeffrey turned. He held a shovel. At his feet was a rectangular mound of earth.

"If I was wrong, I'm sorry. But I thought it was best that I bury him right away."

I nodded.

"I didn't try to find anything to use as a coffin. I thought you might prefer —"

"I do." I wanted that as soon as possible my friend would become grass, and wild poppies, and olive seedlings.

"If you want me to put up some sort of marker —"

I love you. I love you so very much.

For one disconcerting moment I thought I had spoken the words, but of course I hadn't. I said, "A marker wouldn't mean anything to anyone but me, and I won't be here much longer."

He leaned on the shovel, brilliant eyes studying my face. "Then you feel well enough to go to Milan today? I could drive you there in the Simca. After your plane takes off, I can return your car to the rental people, and then take the train back here."

I tried to ignore the twist of pain his words brought me. Of course he wanted me out of his life as soon as possible. No matter how much he liked me, no matter how much he was attracted to me — and I knew he had been attracted to me from the first — he still could not ignore the things I had told him last night. "Poisoned roots," Althea had scribbled on that scrap of paper, and she had been right.

And yet as I'd lain, crying and talking incoherently, with my head pillowed on his shoulder, I had hoped —

I said, "It's kind of you to offer to drive me all that way. But I feel up to driving the car myself."

"Kind?" He gave me a puzzled frown. "Don't you think I *want* to see you aboard that plane? After all, it will be the last time we'll see each other for several weeks. I won't be in the States for those lectures until August."

He paused. "Maybe by then you'll know what you want to do."

"Do?"

"About us. I'm hoping of course that

we'll get married."

I said after a long moment, "Married? You want to marry me?"

"Why that dumfounded look? Surely you must know how I feel, especially after last night. I mean, what does a man have to do to make it clear to you that he loves you?"

I said, past the tight band that seemed to be closing around my throat, "Jeffrey, didn't you hear anything I told you last night? My grandfather was a racketeer who would have gone to prison if he hadn't slipped out of the States. And my sister — my sister was —"

I couldn't go on. He leaned the shovel against a tree trunk, walked over to me, gripped my shoulders, and kissed me soundly on the mouth.

"I wouldn't give a damn," he said, "if your grandfather was Attila the Hun and your sister was Messalina. Now go upstairs and pack your suitcase."

I went upstairs then and packed my suitcase.

The employees of Thorndike Press hope you have enjoyed this Large Print book. All our Large Print titles are designed for easy reading, and all our books are made to last. Other Thorndike Press Large Print books are available at your library, through selected bookstores, or directly from us.

For information about titles, please call:

(800) 223-2336

To share your comments, please write:

Publisher
Thorndike Press
P.O. Box 159
Thorndike, Maine 04986

DATE DUE